BLACK

CW00548798

THE DAMSEL

by
David Dixon

THE DAMSEL

Second Edition Copyright © 2021 by Dark Brew Press

ISBN
Paperback: 978-1-990317-02-6
eBook: 978-1-990317-03-3

Interior design by Crystal L. Kirkham
www.darkbrewpress.com

THE BLACK SUN SERIES

by David Dixon

The Damsel

Six-Gun Shuffle
(*Coming Soon*)

Hell Hath No Fury
(*Coming Soon*)

DAVID DIXON

CHAPTER ONE

People often think of privateering as a lonely business.

You know, flying around from planet to planet, living in spaceports, hotels, being stuck in the cramped confines of a cargo ship. Everybody seems to think it's a job for steely-eyed loners who enjoy their own company, but that's just wrong. In fact, we meet new people all the time. As privateers, the boss and I spend our time jumping from sector to sector, planet to planet, and station to station. Each landing brings a new set of faces, and we almost never work for the same person twice. Not to mention, we've seen the inside of every shitty club and spaceport bar in The Fringe and hit on every waitress, lush, and stripper from Mon Astra to the Tanika Outpost.

We meet plenty of people.

The real problem in our line of work is that the human race is generally made up of assholes, and as such, we privateers meet more than our share. The *reason* we so rarely work for the same people twice is three-quarters of them don't pay in full, and the rest don't pay at all. But to be honest, the people we work for are shining examples of virtue compared to the folks we deal with on a daily basis—the competition, customs officers, corrupt cops, hired guns, drug runners, gangsters, death cults, con-men, and the insane. And, don't even get me started on my boss, though he'd probably say the same about me.

I'd say the ratio of assholes to good people is probably ninety-nine to one. So, when you meet somebody you might actually like in this business, it's a goddamn miracle. Problem is, to meet that one person you like, you gotta deal with a lot of assholes.

This was never truer than during our most recent trip to Ramseur.

I sat in the cockpit trying to remember how to recover the engine's maintenance logs from the central computer when I heard footsteps behind me. I thought nothing of it, since the boss had been back in the cargo bay running tests on the engine coolant trying to figure out if we could squeeze another couple of runs out of it before we had to replace it—that stuff isn't cheap. I figured it was just him coming back up to tell me our savings were going to be wiped out.

Bad news of the typical sort, in other words.

A shadow passed over the main computer terminal. A flash of light exploded inside my skull like fireworks and a thousand blasting trumpets and I found myself smashed face first into the keyboard. My head swam and I tasted blood.

Instinctively, I jerked back and tried to squirm around in the seat to either get away or at least see where the next blow was coming from.

I failed miserably, of course. Instead of dodging the blow, all I did was ensure the next strike caught me in the mouth. It was no softer than the first, and I felt my left incisor split.

That hurt. A lot.

"What the fuck?" I slurred around a busted lip.

I squinted through the pain and saw a blurry silhouette of a short, thin man I didn't recognize.

What I did recognize, though, was the not-at-all-blurry gun barrel staring me in the face.

"Now do what I say or else you're gonna get it again," the man said in a nervous, high-pitched voice. The pistol flicked to the left to indicate the "it" he referred to meant another gun barrel to the head.

"Uh huh." I nodded, trying to focus my eyes through the throbbing crescendo of agony in my head.

Some small part of my brain not concerned with immediately generating and cataloguing all my various types of pain wondered just exactly what was going on. Namely, where *the ever-loving fuck* was my boss and why had he been replaced by the Mad Pistol Whipper here? And, of course, if someone had to get beaten by this guy, why couldn't it have been the boss instead of me?

"Get us out of here," my mysterious assailant ordered.

Just as I was about to object with something completely and perfectly logical like *"Well, I'd love to, asshole, but you see I'm not actually the pilot of this rust bucket, so if you'd like to beat someone senseless so you can get off this godforsaken rock of a planet, I'm perfectly fine with that, but you'll just have to wait until my boss who* is *the pilot gets here and then you can beat him all you want,*" I heard the sound of the boss's boots as he stepped through the airlock threshold that separated the cargo bay from the rest of the ship.

My vision returned and the immediate sharpness of my misery subsided into the gentler type of dull, chronic pain that keeps people up for days and causes them to lose all desire to live. The details of my attacker gradually came into focus, and I had a great view of my boss's face when he looked into the cockpit and saw an armed stranger and saw the stranger's pistol staring him square in the face. It was the sort of incredulous look somebody might have after they've been told they'd just ingested a lethal amount of rat poison.

"Drop that," the mystery man ordered my boss, with a jerk of his pistol to indicate my boss's shoulder rig.

The boss hesitated and our uninvited guest swung the barrel of the gun into my head again. Fireworks exploded in my skull and vomit rose in my throat.

"What was that for?" I whined through clenched teeth, "I'm plenty subdued, hit *him* for fuck's sake."

"Shut up," the high-pitched voice answered as he swung the pistol back toward my boss. He locked eyes with my pistol-wielding tormenter but made no move.

"I said *drop it*." The man's gun went up to between the boss's eyes. Despite this, my boss managed a sidelong glance at me, which told me he was planning something. Somebody was about to get shot.

Both of us, most likely.

"All right, all right, I'm just going to pull it out real slow like. No need to get jumpy here," my boss said calmly while he reached for the .45 in his shoulder holster. As he put his hand on the grip, I saw his pinky finger flick almost imperceptibly.

Halfway twisted around in the pilot's chair as I was, I barely had enough time to throw myself as far as I could over the right-hand armrest and switchboard and smash my head—again—into the navigation display.

It was a good thing I did, because that was all that saved me from taking a .45 round right in the chin.

The boss had his revolver up in a flash, firing at least twice inside the cramped interior of the ship at a target less than eight feet from him. Of course, Snake isn't his nickname, it's mine, so he didn't exactly move with mamba-like speed, which meant our mystery assailant had time to shoot too.

And because this kind of failure is what he excels at, my boss also missed. His two rounds slammed into the back of the pilot's seat where my head had been not a millisecond earlier and through that into the instrument console. There was a ringing in my ears like the world's loudest cymbals, and something warm and wet in my left ear told me I now had a ruptured an eardrum.

Our attacker, meanwhile, had missed also, but had considerably more to show for it than did the boss: in the mad confusion of a gun battle *inside* our already-cramped ship, the boss had backpedaled wildly, tripped over the open turret hatch, and fallen backwards inside it, cracking his head soundly on the outer mag lock ring for good measure before he disappeared down into the turret. Not content to bungle his rescue attempt merely by almost killing me and managing to fall into the most confined space in the craft, my intrepid boss also managed to flail about as he fell and pull an improperly-secured storage locker down with him.

It opened as it fell, spilling a cascade of tools, dirty rags, and a five-gallon bucket of hydraulic fluid into the turret with him. Our mysterious hijacker sprung to the edge of the turret and, without looking, fired two shots down after my companion. Then he slid the turret hatch closed and set the external magnetic safety lock—effectively locking the turret from the outside, so even if my boss and pilot were still alive, he was trapped inside.

When it rains, it pours, and when it pours it's a goddamn monsoon.

I was going to have to get myself out of this without help from my boss, which bummed me out more than it should have, given his already-demonstrated lack of skill in the help department. Bleeding from my ears, nose, and mouth, I was pretty sure my goose was well and fully cooked.

The gunman turned his attention back to me, smoking pistol in his hand.

I decided compliance to be the smartest policy.

Our attacker's voice was now a register higher than it had been before, almost an excited squeak: "Get us out of here!"

"I'm not actually the…" I sighed, realizing the futility of trying to protest. "Fine. *Fine*. You know what? Fuck it, all right?"

This guy wanted me to fly, which meant he couldn't, and trying to explain to him that as the turret gunner I wasn't exactly a pilot in much the same way I wasn't exactly a space ship was going to wind up one of two ways. Either me being shot and him going to hijack somebody else—which I'd have been perfectly fine with except for the being shot part—or him shooting me and trying to fly it himself. Either way, I was a dead man, so I figured being a pilot was my best shot.

How hard could it be?

"All right," I said. "But you two shooting the place up hasn't done much for the ship, so give me a minute before you crack me over the head again, will you?"

"Just get us gone!" he yelled.

I swore under my breath as I looked around me. The cockpit was full of switches, VDUs, buttons, indicator lights, a few analog gauges here and there, and a myriad of taped notes and procedures the boss had left himself. I kind of knew what everything was, but that was different than knowing how to fly the thing.

A ship is like a woman—just because you know what all the parts are doesn't mean you know how to operate them.

The boss had taped his preflight checklist to the left armrest, and I tried to follow it as best I could. Unfortunately, his handwriting was worse than my kindergarten Chinese, and what little I could make out was so dirty and sweat-stained that I wasn't sure if trying to follow the list did more harm than good.

At the very least, I knew how to start the engines. After a little hunting around to verify the ground locks were engaged, I switched the engines on and was rewarded by the satisfying *thump-whine* as they engaged. From there, things got tricky.

I knew, for instance, that a proper preflight included revving them through a full power cycle and checking to see they provided the proper power output at all throttle ranges, but I had no idea how to do this from the cockpit station, and I wasn't even going to bother asking my captor if I could climb back to the cargo bay maintenance panel where I felt more comfortable doing engine work. *Oh well, fuck it*, I thought, *we'll skip making sure the engines actually work—after all, they worked last time, right?*

I flipped all the rocker switches printed *cockpit power*, *communications power*, *life support*, and an array of rocker switches hand-labeled "Crit. Sys. 1" through "Crit. Sys. 4." I must have gotten something out of order, because I got amber warning lights above critical systems two and three. The ship's computer beeped with disapproving tones. I ignored it and flicked a couple of other switches and made a few adjustments I thought looked familiar from when I'd seen the boss do his preflight. The computer *really* didn't like this, which prompted a warning chime and VDU message asking me if I really wanted to start the jump computer core without first turning on the cooling relay.

"What's that noise?" asked the hijacker, now uncomfortably close behind me in the cockpit.

"Nothing," I lied as I cut the jump core computer off. "Just let me do my job and fly, all right?"

In desperation, I looked over the cockpit again, totally lost in the sea of options in front of me, running down a mental list of ship systems in my head before I remembered navigation and targeting. I turned on the navigation suite and was prompted to enter "Local Navsat Magnetic Correction Offset Factor," which I was pretty sure was important but had no idea what it was. I punched in *12345* and hit enter. The computer displayed a bunch of data I knew was incorrect, like showing our altitude at three-hundred-thirty meters above ground level, which was off by a rather critical three-hundred-thirty meters.

I turned my attention to the ship's targeting system. The labels below the switches and buttons had long since been erased by use. Nothing about the layout resembled my station in the turret, but I knew enough to know the cockpit station had all the options I was used to and then some. I turned every switch on the panel to on but didn't press any of the buttons and hoped that was good enough. The radar display was a sea of fuzzy green, but I figured that was just backscatter from the radar being so close to the ground.

"C'mon, c'mon, let's go!" the hijacker said from behind me.

"Look," I said to stall for time as my mind raced to find a way out of the situation that didn't involve me actually trying to fly this thing, "this stuff takes time. Flying through space ain't like…" I didn't know what to compare it to that wasn't cliché, so I just trailed off.

"Get us off the ground or I'm gonna start hitting you again," he warned.

"Fine," I said, wincing.

As I reached for the retro-rocket throttle I noticed an indicator light warning me the rear cargo bay door was open, as was the internal cargo bay hatch, meaning the ship would not pressurize as we flew higher. I entertained a brief notion of trying to fly us up high enough until my assailant passed out, but figured he'd notice the wide-open door and the wind rushing around it and thought better of it.

I had no idea how to close the rear cargo bay door from the cockpit as I usually did it from the maintenance panel just above the turret, but I did know how to close the internal hatch. I pressed the button and the hatch between the crew compartment and cargo bay swung shut.

I increased the throttle to the retro-rockets and the ship lurched drunkenly off the ground and slid forward, scraping the front skid across the pavement, snapping us forward and almost making my assailant lose his balance.

"What the fuck?" the hijacker asked.

I ignored him, tugged gently back on the stick, engaged the retro rockets, and dialed up the anti-grav boosters as I did so, doing my best to imitate what I'd seen my boss do a thousand times. We lifted off—rather smoothly I might add, considering it was my first takeoff under power.

A warning light reminded me the cargo bay door was still open, but being as the internal door wasn't, it wasn't going to hurt anything.

Under anti-grav and retro-rocket power, the ship shuddered its way into Ramseur's upper atmosphere. When the ascent began to slow, I throttled up the ship's primary engines, praying I was up high enough to where they didn't overheat before we got out of the atmosphere.

We punched through a thick cloud layer and out into space. Problem was, I didn't have any idea how to calculate or where to look to know when we'd escaped the planet's gravity well, and an error there would mean the sort of unplanned re-entry that ended with the ship burning up in the atmosphere or screaming into the ocean at meteor-speed. To be safe, I punched the throttle and kept the nose pointed toward the stars.

I decided the best course was to keep on faking it until I could come up with an actual plan, which was about ninety percent of what the boss and I did anyway, so I'd gotten pretty good at it.

CHAPTER TWO

Since I'd just blasted off without clearance and no declared flight path, I had expected several calls from the tower and Ramseur authorities. The fact that I hadn't heard anything meant the comm settings must have been wrong, which wouldn't have been such a big deal had it not also meant I had no way to call for help.

I pulled up the autopilot on the main VDU and skimmed through the options presented to me. I pressed the menu button labeled "route to nearest nav beacon." The ship's computer chimed and I heard the engine thrust levels change. I took that as a good sign. Unfortunately, it was accompanied by several warning lights on the navigation console, which I took to be a bad sign. I shrugged it off, figuring I'd be dead long before whatever catastrophe they were trying to warn me about happened anyway.

"All right," I said, looking over my handiwork. "We're off planet. Now, I'm going to turn around so I can talk to you, all right?"

"Don't turn around!" the voice ordered. "Your buddy tried that with me and look where he wound up."

I stifled the urge to scream something at this asshole for reminding me, *thank you very much*, that he'd probably just offed my only friend. Instead, I bit my tongue and nodded.

"Okay," I answered evenly, staring out into the blackness of space through the cockpit windscreen and gathering my thoughts. "Fine. Just tell me this—what the hell do you want me to do now?"

"I want to get off world," the hijacker answered.

"Done," I pointed out. "Now what?"

"I want to go to…" The voice trailed off.

I gritted my teeth.

This guy hadn't even figured out where he wanted to go before he hijacked a jump capable cargo ship, shot its pilot, then blasted off world with an untrained stand in?

Great. Just fucking *awesome*.

"I want to go to, uh," the hijacker continued, "to… to Paris V. Yeah, man, Paris V."

Paris V was a trendy place, with loads of casinos, hotels, resorts, and girls—as long as you had stacks of cash to pay for it all, which I had to guess did *not* describe someone who would hijack a Black Sun 490.

"What are you gonna do there?" I asked. "Because unless you got a duffel bag full of cash you dropped off in the hold or a Seven Suns Black Card in your wallet, you ain't gonna find shit to do on Paris V."

I neglected to mention that since I still hadn't closed the cargo bay door, if he *had* had a duffel bag full of credits in the hold, he didn't have it there any longer. I just wished the ship's safety system didn't prevent me from opening the internal hatch when the outer door was open. If it didn't, I would have just strapped myself in, opened the door and vented the cabin and him with it before closing the door and letting the ship automatically re-pressurize.

As I dreamt about turning his body into a frozen chunk of human space junk, he prattled on. "Paris

V is gonna be fucking awesome. I'm gonna go score me some cash at The Louvre and then go score with some girls at Moulin Rouge. Then, I'm—"

"What do you think The Louvre is? A charity? It's a fucking *casino*, and a high roller one at that. You don't go to casinos to *make* money. You go there if you've already *got* money. Like I said, unless you're a lot richer than I think, two days after you hit Paris V, you're gonna find yourself in some ratty hostel off Rue du Seine turning tricks for cash. Did you not listen to a word I said about Paris V?"

"Uh, yeah, okay, fine." He didn't say anything for a moment until he piped up with his next bright idea. "Well, what about New Reno?"

I put my head in my hands. The only thing worse than a hijacker with a plan, it seemed, was a hijacker *without* one.

"Have you ever been off world? Anywhere?" I asked.

"What difference does that make?" he said.

Something about his tone set me off. I risked a look back at him. He sat atop the turret hatch, knees drawn up, pistol between them, casually pointed at my back. Despite my pounding headache from the earlier beating I'd taken, one look at him was all it took for everything to fall into place.

The guy was a kid—maybe nineteen at the oldest, but his trendy blonde spiky haircut, designer shoes, and name-brand shirt marked him as probably even younger. Where he'd gotten the gun, I hadn't the foggiest, but his lack of scars made it obvious he wasn't a career criminal or street tough. He was far too defensive and too impulsive to have been at this very long.

He was also too dumb, since he'd hijacked a ship as obviously shitty as ours. I figured he must not have understood that since hijacking ships is a good way to get killed, most of the folk who do it professionally hijack the *best* ships rather than the worst ones, and not just because the worst ones aren't worth anything. It's really because the worst ships are unsafe, and, crewed by people with nothing to lose who would think nothing of gunning you down the first chance they got.

People like me, in other words.

Furthermore, since the first two places he'd picked to go when his harebrained scheme had been an unexpected success had been two places popular on the holos, I guessed this was his only exposure to off-world life, which meant he was going to be in for a rude awakening when he got exposed to the ninety-nine point ninety-nine percent of the rest of the universe that wasn't nearly as pleasant as Paris V and New Reno were made out to be.

The kid was an amateur who didn't realize just how much of an amateur he was, which made him very, very dangerous indeed, like a baby viper who couldn't control his venom.

I sighed. "Look, kid—"

"Don't call me kid," he snapped.

"Fine," I agreed with a shrug, "I won't, but listen to me. You are making a huge mistake. First, you've hijacked a spacecraft, which even your dumb ass probably doesn't need me to tell you is a capital offense, *and* you got no way to fly if you kill me, which is probably what you think you'd like to do. You've also got no money, which means even if you do manage to get someplace, you can't do anything once you get there. Did I miss anything?"

The kid sneered, "I don't need your fuckin' analysis, okay? I'm the one with the gun. What's going to happen is you're gonna fly me where I tell you to, then I'm going to kill you and sell this ship for cash. How's that?"

I rolled my eyes. "I did miss something, actually. You got shit for brains. Since you've just told me you're going to kill me anyway, why the fuck should I do what you tell me to? Also, by the way, I'd love to see you try to offload this ship without a title or seller's license. You can't even—"

"I can too. There are lots of ways to—"

"Yeah, kid, it can be done, because I've done it," I snapped. "But the kind of people who help you do that sort of thing would take one look at you and shoot you dead on the spot rather than take the trouble to buy it off of you. Or, likely as not, they wouldn't, because this rustbucket is worth about as much as your shoes and wouldn't be worth killing you for, much less *paying* you for."

For once in my life, I wished I was facing up against a smart crook instead of a stupid one.

"So, here's a new plan for you, kid," I snarled. "You let me take this crate back down to Ramseur, I kick you off and I take my friend to the hospital on the double quick. Meanwhile, you pray he isn't dead and doesn't get that way, or else I come by your house in the middle of the night and gut your entire goddamn family. Sound good?"

The kid flinched.

The possibility of my boss being dead had really started to sink in, and I felt the return of an anger I hadn't felt since my *Braxton* years so long ago.

"No!" shouted the kid, voice high and quivering. "You're just trying to scare me and tell me what to do. Fuck that. I'm in charge here—I got the gun, so you listen to me!"

I shrugged. "Fine, kid, but that was your last chance. This thing may end badly for me, but I straight up *guarantee* this is going to end badly for you."

I turned back around to check the cockpit and see if any new warning lights had come on.

Several had, but something else entirely caught my eye: the maintenance log. It looked much like it always did, with time stamped records of ship processes turning on and off, relays operating, and sensor readings, with one major exception. At the bottom of the log, a message stared at me.

///10.23.1114.01 – Relay XB889: ON 01.01.02

///10.23.1114.02 –Radiation Sensor Set 94B DETECT OFF

///10.23.1114.03 –909011.2 mBUS FAULT

///10.23.1114.04 –where are we

The boss was alive, and somehow, he now was typing in the maintenance log. I figured he must be appending a note to one of the sensor relays in the turret, which I knew was possible, but I'd never done.

The *where are we* message repeated.

I fiddled around with the keyboard and VDU until I saw the option come up on screen to "Create

Maintenance Data Note." I typed back: *don't know nav computer broken but on autopilot to nearest nav beacon*.

The response wasn't exactly what I'd hoped for. I was looking for a way out of this mess or perhaps a congratulations for not smashing us into the ground on my first-ever flight. Instead, I got *wrong correction factor so nav computer is steering us wrong look out the window idiot*.

I did so and realized that instead of heading toward a nav beacon, the ship instead headed toward what appeared to be a small asteroid belt. I grimaced and pulled gently left on the stick to try to steer us toward where I thought the nav beacon would be. Nothing happened.

I swore silently as I typed *can't steer ship*.

I could almost hear his insulting tone through the maintenance log: *disengage autopilot maybe?*

I flipped a few switches until the autopilot disengaged. I swung the ship around as slowly as I could, but the maneuver did not escape the attention of our hijacker.

"Hey," he said. "I didn't tell you to change course."

"Yeah? You also never told me what course to take, so unless you want to fly into an asteroid field, you'd better let me get us headed toward a nav beacon."

"Get us to the jump point," he ordered. "We're going to New Reno."

"All right," I said, even though I had no idea how to get us to the jump point and even less of a clue how to jump.

I pointed the ship in the same direction as the pinpricks of light I knew to be other crafts' running lights, although the targeting computer still showed all green so I couldn't tell what size or type they were.

There was another maintenance message from the boss: *good job steering this is sarcasm btw.*

I scowled as I typed back *glad to see you aren't hurt also sarcasm.*

His next message was more useful: *fuse relays showing rear cargo door open, is that right?*

I knew what he was thinking. I smiled. I typed back *yes but safety won't let me open inner door while outer is open b/c pressure diff.*

"What are you typing on so much up there?" the hijacker asked.

I hate it when people rudely interrupt discussions of what's the best way to kill them.

"Well, I'm going through the ship's maintenance data trying to figure out what's going on," I lied. "Remember those gunshots in the cabin? Remember the coupl'a shots that missed you and gave me this?" I put a finger up to my bloody-and-still-ringing ear. "Those two rounds went in here." I pointed to the two bullet holes in the center console, which I was pretty sure hadn't hit anything more important than the cockpit's windshield defroster. "Those two shots have done some pretty major damage to a mainboard or two, and I'm trying to figure out how to reroute stuff so I can get all the systems back up."

"Can we jump?" was all he wanted to know.

I shrugged.

The real answer was *not really*, but it had nothing to do with the gunshots and everything to do with the fact I had no clue how to calculate a jump, but there was no point in telling him that.

"Sure, we can, kid." I kept the lie train rolling smartly down the tracks. "'Cept, we don't have comms, and that might make things a bit tricky when in-system wants to scan us before we leave your lovely home system here, don't ya think?"

I craned my neck around to see if the very sensible thing I had just told him had sunk in, hoping perhaps he would abandon this colossally stupid enterprise.

No such luck.

Instead, he doubled down on his lunacy. "Just burn past insys and hit the jump point."

I sighed. I needed to get rid of this kid before one of his bright ideas did it for all of us.

"Look, genius, I dunno if you paid any attention to the ship you chose to hijack before you came in here swinging that pistol upside my head and shooting the place up, but this is a cargo hauler, and an old one at that. This thing isn't a fighter and it ain't a combat shuttle and it ain't a corvette. This isn't the holos, guy. I try to pull a stunt like that—with my turret locked down, no less—and insys will hull us no sweat."

"I'm getting tired of your excuses," the kid snapped. "People burn past patrols all the time."

I turned all the way around to face him. "Yeah, they do. In the *movies*, you dumb shit, but try that in real life and we'll be sucking vacuum before we get close to the jump point. Even piece of shit little planets like Ramseur—which would have to be quite a piece of shit indeed to produce someone as epically fucked up as you are—have insys fighters with *missiles*, something which I realize in the holos pose little danger, but pose significantly more danger when you're in a tin can like this one and they're actually shooting them at you. Guess how many missiles we'll take at full shields?" I asked him, giving him a sardonic smile.

He shrugged, scowling like a spoiled brat who'd just been told he was up past his bedtime.

"Try zero," I offered. "That's right—*not a fucking one.* Even at full shields, a single insys imrec will turn us inside out." I tapped the cockpit windshield.

"So," I continued in as calm a voice as I could muster, "how about you just let me work out the comms issue while you sit back there and keep your finger off the trigger so you don't accidentally shoot me in the back of the head, okay?"

When I turned back around, the boss had a message waiting for me in the log: *i disabled door safety to rear panel but cockpit safety is on different system.*

I considered that a moment. So, the door safety switch at the cockpit still wouldn't let me open it, but the rear panel just above the turret hatch now had the safety disabled, meaning if I could somehow get back there to my usual station and flip the switch, the door located not three feet from that switch would open and vent the cabin out into space.

Which was great, except one *tiny* detail. Namely, venting the cabin would also vent me right out as well, leaving no one to close the hatch. But if somehow, I could make it back up to the cockpit, I could hit the switch at the cockpit station and close the hatch again, because if the ship sensed a sudden depressurization, the cockpit safety would disengage and allow the hatch to be shut.

I knew this because we'd had an incident where the boss had forgotten the hold was unpressurized, although the rear cargo door was closed. When I'd opened the internal hold hatch the resulting air pressure equalization had almost blown my eardrums out before my boss closed the door from his station.

I hadn't forgotten or forgiven him for that.

For the next few minutes, I tried to figure out how I was going to leap from the cockpit across our hijacker to the switch, flip it, and then leap back to the cockpit without being shot first or sucked out into the void second.

Then it hit me.

I typed a quick message to the boss: *hold onto your hat*.

I pretended to focus on the targeting computer. Then I made a show of flipping a switch and swearing under my breath.

"What's going on?" the kid asked.

"Uh oh, kid, bad news—real bad," I told him.

"What? What is it? What do you mean bad news?"

"I got an insys tail—that kind of bad news," I lied, trying my best to sound scared.

"What do you mean?"

"I mean insys has probably been trying to contact me ever since you had me blast off-world without clearance. Since I haven't said a word in response, they must figure I'm up to something, so they're out behind me at about ten thousand klicks."

The kid was silent for a second while all that sunk in. "They're gonna shoot us?"

I resisted the urge to scream *"No, you idiot, voice comms go out all the time and you just use Morse code with your running lights to communicate like people have been doing for like eight hundred years"* but I decided giving him a useful little bit of spacefaring knowledge would be a waste of breath since I was planning on spacing him in a minute anyway.

Instead, I responded with all the false worry I could muster in my voice. "Uh, yeah, they'll probably start shooting soon if they don't hear from us."

I was kind of halfway hoping the kid would start crying or begging for his mom, which would lead to a quiet surrender of his firearm, but I'll admit I was wickedly pleased with the stupidity of his response.

"Don't try to pull one on me now," he warned me with a squeak of false bravado. "You're just trying to get insys to board us. I'm not falling for that. You're gonna fight him off or die trying."

I could barely contain my glee but tried to sound as desperate as I could. "Uh, okay, kid but… this ship, if you didn't notice, is a two man operation, see, and since you shot my dude earlier, there's nobody to man the turret, which means fighting isn't much of an option."

I trailed off and left the bait in the water, waiting for him to strike.

Five seconds passed before he took it.

"I can man it," he told me in a statement of such massive ignorance it's a wonder it didn't create a point of infinite ignorance mass and density and form a black hole of ignorance, ending all life in the system.

It was just the kind of stupidity I was counting on.

Before I could answer, I noticed another message from the turret: *no way*. Apparently, my boss had his ear pressed to the turret hatch and had gathered the drift of my plan.

I wiped the grin off my face before I turned back to face the hijacker. "You *sure* you can man that turret?" I asked. "I dunno, but like you say, you're the one with the gun. Thing is, you mag-locked it earlier. Open the switch box there." I pointed at the rear maintenance panel right next to him. "And count three switches in."

He flipped open the maintenance cover and counted three switches to the red rocker switch under a protective plastic cover. He pointed to the switch, apparently unconcerned about the fact it had *DANGER* written in big red letters across the cover.

"That one?"

I pretended it was no big deal. "Uh-huh, that one."

He opened the cover and flipped the switch.

There was a bang like a bomb blast as the internal crew compartment/bay door slid open and the ship explosively depressurized. The pressure loss ripped the air from my lungs and snapped my head back fast enough to give me whiplash. I felt blood vessels popping and thought my eyes were going to bulge out of my head.

For half an instant, me and the kid locked eyes—mine cruelly triumphant and his wide in panic—before he vanished out the hatch, through the cargo bay, and into the void.

I smashed the hatch button in the cockpit and the hatch slammed shut with a resounding clash of steel. The ship's life support system roared for a second to replace all the lost atmosphere, and I could breathe again.

I gasped, heart pounding and head throbbing. After a few seconds' rest, I let myself out of the cockpit and kicked the mag release switch with my foot. The hatch slid open and the boss stared up at me from inside the turret.

"Sweet mother of Jesus, Snake, you talked him into spacing *himself*. Fuckin' awesome. Remind me not to cross you, eh?"

I nodded weakly. In the absence of adrenaline, I now felt every strike our unwelcome visitor had laid on me.

I jerked a thumb toward the cockpit.

"You," I told him, "out of the turret and up there. I'm done for the day. It's all I can do to fix this crate *and* shoot well enough to keep us alive despite your dodgy piloting, but I now gotta to *fly* it too?"

"Trust me," he said as he climbed out of the turret and squeezed past me. "I'd much rather be up there than in here. God only knows what you fucked up, up there."

I ignored him as I dropped down inside and settled into my familiar cramped quarters and lit a much-needed cigarette. "What in Jesus fuck were you doing back there when he came on board? Did you just wave to him as he waltzed in right past you?" Before he had a chance to answer, I cut him off. "And what's with the crazy gun ninja moves, bro? You nearly shot my damn head off!"

"I didn't see him," he answered as he settled into his seat. "I was checking the level in the aft hydraulic tank and he must have walked right past without seeing me."

"Well, next time, how about you pay a little more attention?" I groused.

"I almost got shot too, you know," he reminded me. "When he fired down through the turret hatch, I felt the wind as the rounds went past."

"My heart bleeds for you," I said. "And so do my teeth, and my ear, and my lip. Now get us back down to Ramseur. I'm going to sleep."

I got comfortable and closed my eyes.

From above, I heard a cascade of profanity from the boss. "Snake, what the hell did you do? Did you turn the targeting radar on full power *on the ground?* You fried the receiver dome!"

Without opening my eyes, I raised my right hand and extended my middle finger.

"I'm still a better pilot than you are, and if you've got a problem with it, just flip the third switch from the end, would you?"

CHAPTER THREE

The next afternoon, we stood looking at the Black Sun 490's targeting system receiver dome. We'd spent the entire morning getting the cover off, resetting the system, replacing two of the transistors with spares, and generally trying to get the array to show anything but a waterfall of green static. We were tired, hungry, and getting nowhere, and I still had a splitting headache from the previous day's misadventures.

The boss scowled as he looked up from the laptop plugged into the radar's auxiliary data-port.

"Nope. Still nothing. The whole fucking array's going to have to be replaced."

"I've done this before, man, I'm telling you, when I was on the *Wang Fu*," I said. "Last time, all I did was replace the magnetrons, reset the—"

He cut me off with a wave of his hand. "And I'm telling you, *again*, this isn't a passively scanned array. For the fiftieth time, there is no goddamn magnetron to replace. You looking for the magnetron on an actively scanned array is like me looking for your brain—there's no point in looking for something that was never there in the first place."

"You're just pissed off because you think it's my fault," I said.

"As I see it, it pretty much is."

"I'm not the pilot, how was I supposed to know?"

"Why'd you turn it on in the first place?" he asked, stabbing an angry finger at the radar array. "You didn't need targeting. You weren't going to duke it out with anybody. You should have just left it off if you didn't know what you were doing."

"You say that now," I said, "but me not knowing what I was doing applies to pretty much everything I did yesterday, which, I'd just like to note, ended with us in one piece solely due to my quick thinking, so I don't want to hear any bullshit from you. It's just as much your fault as it is mine, 'cause if you'd have been paying more attention in the first place, he wouldn't have been able to sneak aboard and threaten to shoot me if I didn't figure out real quick how to fly this piece of space salvage."

The boss didn't answer. Instead, he shut his laptop and yanked the cable out of the auxiliary jack. He stomped off toward the forward hatch.

"Hey, where are you going?" I called.

"To lock up the laptop. Fuck the radar. It's time for a drink."

I looked uncertainly at the exposed receiver.

"Don't we need to put the cover back on? I don't think it's supposed to be out in the weather."

"Why bother?" he said as he closed and locked our Black Sun's forward hatch. "A little rain won't hurt it. It's shot anyway."

I shrugged and followed him off the landing pad and toward the tram station that would take us into the Ramseur Spaceport's commerce district.

An hour later we sat at a cramped table at The Circuit, a crowded shipper's bar full of privateers like ourselves, a few insys rat runners, working girls, drunk asteroid miners, and some union boys with patches that said *Shipper's Local 301* who nursed their beers while giving the rest of us the evil eye. The music was shitty and whatever the popular local blend of tobacco was smelled to high heaven, but the beer was good, which was what really mattered, at the moment.

I scrolled through the local listings using the built-in tabletop screen on my side of the table, smoking a cigarette in violation of the no-smoking sign, and looking for anybody who might have a job for us. On his side of the table, the boss scanned through prices for replacement radar arrays and his expression grew sourer as he scrolled. Finally, he sighed, leaned back, and finished off his beer.

"See anything?" he asked.

"Nah. Not much. Some stuff out there for bid but it's all too big. Oversize cargo, high volume bulk agriculture, that kind of thing."

"Shit."

"Yeah," I said. "What about you? Any luck on the radar replacement?"

"Twelve thou at the low end, and that's used. And it's at Ringo's," he added.

"Ringo? That motherfucker's so crooked he can't even piss in a straight line," I muttered. "If we buy it from him, I doubt it'll work any better than the one we've already got."

He grunted. "That's a given. It's either that, or the system is still installed in some poor sap's ship who isn't gonna know it's for sale until he wakes up one morning and finds it gone."

"Okay, so assuming we don't get it from Ringo, how much are we talking?"

"Looks like the going rate is about seventeen k," the boss answered as he checked the table again. "Which is about twelve grand more than I've got in the account right now, by the way."

"I suppose I could loan you some of it," I offered, hiding my smirk behind my beer.

"You could loan *me* some of it?" he asked, incredulously. "Motherfucker, I should dock it from your pay. You're gonna loan *me* some money. That's a good one."

At the mention of him docking my pay, my smile disappeared. "You'd have to actually pay me a wage before you could dock it. I haven't been paid in months," I pointed out.

"Uh huh. And who buys all the food you eat on board? Who pays for all the docking fees and hotel rooms and even the beer most of the time?" he asked.

I shrugged. It was a fair point.

"What would you spend it on anyway?" he asked.

"Booze, most likely."

The boss nodded and signaled for two more beers, which the waiter promptly sat in front of us.

"Ta-da," he said. "Your paycheck."

"What's the legal definition of *indenture*?" I asked. But I still drank the beer.

"I dunno," he shot back. "What's the legal definition of *dependent*?"

"Har har."

I sipped my beer and refreshed the list.

"Anything?" he asked.

"Another refresh and… nope, still nothing," I answered.

"Shit. This is depressing," the boss said.

"You're telling me. Just face it, there's not going to—" I refreshed again, and a new listing caught my eye. "Wait a minute. This might be us. Load of medical supplies out to Preslav. That's only what, three or four days from here? Pays five grand. Not too bad."

He shook his head. "Nope. Preslav is outside federated space. And, if memory serves, there's a civil war on down there."

"There is. Which is probably why they need the medical supplies," I answered. "But who cares if it's outside UNF control? The civil war is planetside. It would be a quick run in and out."

"We don't have a targeting radar, remember, Snake? UNF space is dangerous enough, already, without a radar, and I'm sure as hell not flying *outside* it without one."

"I don't know what's gonna come our way that's gonna be any better," I said and took another swig of my beer.

"How about that for better?" the boss said, with a nod toward the door.

I turned around in my seat. When I saw what he meant, I couldn't help but roll my eyes. It's the same every time with him.

She was a pretty, petite brunette in her early twenties. I say brunette, but that was really more of a guess based on the roots, because her straight, chin-length hair was dyed a faded purple. Her olive skin marked both her mixed ethnicity and her birthplace—somewhere on the outer edge of federated space. Her near-skin-tight flight suit was drab green and unzipped to reveal the faintest hint of cleavage, and the long duster she wore didn't hide her athletic figure any more than it did the pistol she had on her right hip. There was defiance in her step and a glint of purpose in her eye as she surveyed the bar. She was a holo-producer's idea of a mercenary bad-girl.

In short, she looked like trouble, which as far as I could tell seemed to be my boss's favorite attribute in a woman.

"Hey, you, Mr. Empty Wallet, hello," I said to him, tapping the table between us. "Keep your eyes down here looking for radars. I see what you're looking at over there. Don't get any wild ideas. We don't have the money or the time it would take for you to score with her."

He didn't stop watching her as he took another sip of his beer. "I dunno, Snake, I think she might have something for me."

I snorted. "What's that? An STD? A restraining order? A swift kick to the low hanging fruit?"

"No," he said as he got up from the table. "A job."

"Say what?"

"Look," he said with a nod. "She's typing something in at her table. I'm telling you; she's posting a job."

"Who the fuck cares? Even if she is, you don't know what it's gonna be. It could be anything."

"I'ma go check that out," he said as he sauntered over to where she sat.

"Yeah, you do that," I called. "Just make sure you bounce any great ideas she gives you off me. Something about her smells like us getting shot at."

He ignored me.

I scanned the page again but her ad—if it even existed—hadn't shown up yet. I finished my beer and glanced over in my employer's direction. The woman wore a scowl and seemed to be backing away from him, her hand resting dangerously close to her pistol. I shrugged. Overall, he seemed to be doing about as well as he usually did with the fairer sex—on fire and spiraling out of the sky.

I stood and headed toward them, hoping to get a front row seat to what I figured was going to be either a very public rejection or a very public ass kicking and maybe both. The boss noticed me and nodded to me and then looked back at her. I think he thought I was coming to back him up.

I leaned against a nearby post, fished out a cigarette, lit it, and waited for the fireworks. My boss looked over his shoulder and noticed the line of shippers behind him, waiting, I figured, to try their luck at getting whatever she had to offer, job or otherwise. I chuckled.

She stuck out her hand, which he shook.
Oh fuck no.

I cleared the distance between us in a second, parting the crowd like an angry bull.

"This is Snake, my gunner, and we—" the boss said.

"Whoa, whoa," I interrupted. "I don't know what just got agreed to here, but—"

She looked me up and down before arching an eyebrow at the boss. "You were saying?"

"Fuck what *he* was saying," I snapped. "What *I* was saying is whatever you two just shook on as a deal, ain't, because I don't know anything about it."

"So, who works for who again?" she asked the boss in a mocking tone.

He gave me a glare that could have curdled milk. "Don't get it twisted. He works for me. He'll be fine, Carla, just give—"

"The fuck I will," I exploded. "I'm not fine with shit until I know what we're doing. Here's the deal, *Carla*. You tell me exactly what you told him and—"

"You need to get your gunner under control, captain," she told the boss.

I wanted to wring her pretty little neck.

"*You* need to watch it," I snapped.

"Your gunner's quite the feisty one, isn't he," Carla said to the boss with a nod in my direction. "That makes two of us. This ought to be fun. Bang

44

us together and watch the sparks fly." She gave me a sly smile which told me her choice of words wasn't an accident.

I have to admit, usually I'd have been all over an obvious double entendre like that coming from a girl like her, but since she was in the process of roping my boss into what was no doubt going to be the last mission of our lives, I had to let it pass.

"That shit isn't gonna work on me," I said. "So, start talking. What the hell are you trying to get us into?"

She stared across the table at the boss as she unzipped her flight suit—which I admit helped to defuse the tension a bit—to withdraw a pack of cigarettes. "Well?" she asked the boss. "You gonna explain it to him? I made the deal with you, so as far as I'm concerned, this asshole is your problem."

"It's a cargo run," he said. "We leave two days from now. No biggie. She's going to escort us out there and we'll pick it up." I could tell by his roundabout explanation he was dancing around whatever the real issue was. "Our cut is fifteen k. Simple, really. We're just gonna do the Tellison-Markins run and—"

I stabbed a finger in his face. "The Tellison-Markins run? Stop *right* there," I warned him. "I literally cannot believe what I'm hearing right now.

This is the dumbest thing you've ever signed us up for, and you have signed us up for some of the stupidest jobs in the whole damn galaxy. Don't you get it? There's no fucking cargo, dipshit, and there's not gonna be any fifteen grand either, because she knows we won't live to collect. We're *bait*, Boss! Just like she is, coming in here dressed up like a *femme fatale* to try to find some sad, undersexed clown like you to fall for her and agree to her bullshit."

"If you can't do the deal, I'm sure there's plenty of people who can," Carla told the boss as she nodded to the men orbiting the table around us.

"Well, we do need to—" he began.

I sensed his uncertainty, so I decided to interrupt and make sure he didn't jump off the ledge. "Ten minutes ago, you said it was too dangerous to do a fucking milk run to Preslav," I reminded him. "And now you're just gonna sign us up to bebop on through the most notorious route in the quadrant? What sense does that make?"

Carla's eyes narrowed. "Wait a minute," she said. "The run to *Preslav* was too dangerous? What are you flying?" she asked the boss.

"It's a Black Sun 490," he told her, literally puffing out his chest. "An oldie but a goodie, you know. They're super reliable," he lied. "And ours is—"

"Ours is half rusted out and the other half is shot to shit," I interrupted. "*And* our targeting array is on the fritz, so…"

She ignored me, which I found infuriating, and did the eyebrow thing at him again. "So, which is it, flyboy? You gonna do this or not? Because like I said—if you aren't hard enough for this job, I can find somebody who is. This is going to be a hell of a lot worse than a run to Preslav."

For a half a second, I hoped her admission would make my boss see reason, but when I saw her pretty little red tongue come out and flick across those soft pink lips, I knew we were done for.

"No, no, I—we—can do it," the boss stammered, eyes glued to her face. "No sweat. No problem at all. Nav point two in two days at 1400, you said, right? We'll be there, comm channel six zero five."

"Good," she said. "You'd better be."

She slid off her barstool and started to leave. My boss reached for her arm as if to slow her, but she stopped him with a glare which could have frozen a star. He jerked his hand back like he'd just touched a hot stove.

"Don't, you, uh… Do you want a beer?" he asked.

"No."

She strode out of the bar, every male eye but mine trailing her.

For my part, I was staring daggers at my boss and wanting to punch his stupid face in.

CHAPTER FOUR

The next two days went by quickly and quietly. I did my work—recalibrating the turret, replacing the number two laser capacitor and changing out the aft hydraulic pump, while the boss did his—a coolant purge and refill, updating the main computer software, and replacing the forward starboard radiation shield. After the first four or five times I answered his questions with "fuck you," he quit asking me things, which was fine by me.

We were sitting on the tarmac, twenty-sixth in line for takeoff, before I was finally ready to talk again.

"So," I said from the turret, "what's the big plan when we get jumped? 'Cause you know we're gonna get jumped."

"Glad to see you're gonna be a big boy about this and start talking again," he answered.

"Fuck you."

I heard him sigh from the cockpit.

"No, that was just my response to your smartass comment," I said. "It wasn't a fuck you like all the previous fuck yous where you really deserved it for being a fucking fuckhead."

"You know what?" he mused. "I'm gonna buy you a vocabulary book, Snake, so you can learn some new words."

"Oh, is that a fact? I know plenty of vocabulary words. Want to hear 'em?"

"No, not real—"

"Let's see... *fuckhead, fuckface, fuckstick, fucknut, fuckwit*—"

"*Fuckmuch?*" the boss interrupted from the cockpit.

"—*Fucktard*," I continued. "Wait. Did you just say *fuckmuch?*"

"Uh, maybe, yeah," he said. "I guess I did."

"And just what the hell is a *fuckmuch*?" I asked.

"I dunno, it just seemed to fit."

"No. No it does not," I said. "Because all of those other things are words that describe you, and *fuck much* or anything that sounds even remotely close does not describe you."

"How about I come down and *fuckstomp* that shit-eating grin off your face?" he asked.

"Now *that's* the spirit," I said with a chuckle. "But don't think I'm not still pissed. Your infatuation is gonna get us killed. You think that girl is sex on legs, but I'm telling you, she's just bad news in a flight suit."

"Her name is Carla," he corrected me. "And I took the job because of the job, not because of her. I would'a taken it from anybody."

"Come off it," I said. "That's more bullshit than a hold full of steers with diarrhea. You wouldn't have even considered it if it weren't for the fact she's cute as all hell and her flight suit's a size too small. And when she licked her lips? Christ, she had you eating out of her hand."

"You're just jealous," he said.

"Say *what*? What's there to be jealous of?"

"She never even talked to you last night, Snake. She's got eyes only for me, and I know that drives you up the wall. I'm telling you; she's got something for me."

I laughed—not chuckled, not smiled, but straight up *laughed*.

"You're outta your mind, Bossman. First, she was trying to flirt with *me*. Second, didn't you see the ice queen look she gave you when you asked about a beer? She wants *fuck nothing* to do with you. But now I really hope we live through this mission because I can't *wait* to see you try to put some more moves on her."

"You know what your problem is, Snake?" I could tell he'd turned around in his seat to talk to the turret—I must have really gotten to him.

"No, but I'm sure you're gonna tell me," I said.

"Your problem is that you always think you know what women are thinking. You're always telling me 'no, she doesn't like you' or 'she's way out of your league' or 'she wouldn't talk to you even if you bought her the whole bar.' But that's bullshit. You don't know what they're thinking, and you don't know what they're gonna do, either."

"Have I ever been wrong?" I asked, a self-satisfied grin on my face.

"Well… um… actually, *yes*. Yes, you have been," he answered.

"When?"

"Nasra. On Dunbar. Remember Nasra?" he asked. "We'd just picked up a load of Gur Ji Kesk wine and we went to that club? What was it? The Silver Peach or something? You said I had no chance with her, but the only reason she didn't come back with me was we'd already checked out of the hotel. Remember? Because we had such an early departure time the next day? So, we slept on the ship that night, remember?"

In the turret, I pondered whether to prove him wrong or get myself in trouble. I decided to split the difference.

"Maybe that's what she told you, Boss, but even if we had hotel rooms, she wasn't going back with you — *trust me*."

"There you go again, Snake. How would you know?"

"She told me."

"Bullshit. I was with her like the whole night. The only time I left her with you was to go get a drink, and that took like three minutes. There's no way she just looked at you after I left and said, 'I'm not going home with your buddy.' No fuckin' way she did that."

"No, not then," I said. "Later."

I winced, realizing what I'd just done.

"Later?" he asked, puzzled. "There was no 'later,' Snake. We hung out at the club for a bit, but we had such an early day the next morning, we went back to the ship. That was the night it raining like crazy and we found out we had that leaky seal, remember? So, you went out to get a new one."

In the turret, I held my breath, wondering how long it was going to take him.

"And then," he continued, "you called me at like midnight saying you'd lost your shipyard badge so you couldn't get back into the…" His voice trailed off.

In the quiet, I could practically hear the wheels turning in his head.

I coughed to break up the silence.

"Fuck you, man," he said in a small voice.

"Look, it was—"

"No, seriously, Snake, fuck you! You slept with my girl!"

"No," I said matter-of-factly, "she was not your girl. She made that *very* clear—in a variety of ways—which is how I know she wasn't your girl. And how I know she was not going to get with you, even if you did have a room."

"I hate you," he announced.

"Hey, man, you know what? I'm sorry. Really, I am. It was a low-down thing to do, even for a guy named Snake. And it wasn't even that good anyway."

"You know what, Snake? I hope your dick falls off. I really do."

"Aww, c'mon, Boss. That was a long time ago. It was—"

"It was six fucking weeks ago, asshole!" he shouted.

"That's a long time. To some people, I mean."

"Tell you what," my boss said. "Let's just go back to fuck yous for a while, okay?"

"Look, if we live through this, let's just fly back to Dunbar and you can have another shot with her, all right? I promise I'll even stay on the ship the whole—"

"Fuck you, Snake."

━━━━━━━━━━━━━━━

I'm not sure what I expected we would find at nav point two, but whatever it was, it wasn't what we found. Just outside the nav lane, powered down and almost invisible except for running lights, hung a Razor combat shuttle. The ship's sharp, radar-defeating angles couldn't help but give it a menacing look, and whoever owned this one had gone the extra mile, painting it a flat black, with only two dark gray lines down one wing for decoration. My estimation of Carla went up several notches.

"Holy shit. Is that her? I knew they sold 'em, but I've never seen a civilian Razor before," I said, marveling at the ship. "Where the fuck did she get the cash for *that*?"

"Fuck you, Snake. Maybe she got lucky at an auction or something. Everything isn't some sort of goddamned conspiracy."

"No. I'll tell you how she got it," I said. "Shadiness. She's up to something and she has been for a while, just like I told you back in the bar. We'll be lucky if she doesn't wind up turning that thing on us by the time this is over."

"Quit your bitching, Snake. Everything is going to be fine."

"That statement is the opposite of reassuring," I said. "The surest way for things to go wrong is for you to say they're going to be fine. It's like you're some sort of cosmic inverter and whenever you say things are going to be one way, the universe flips to make sure things are the opposite."

"Shut. Up."

Carla's voice came across comm channel six zero five: "You're late."

I looked at my watch. Indeed, we were fifteen minutes behind schedule.

"No biggie," the boss replied. "Lot of traffic. We had to wait for clearance."

"I wasn't sure you'd come," she said. "I didn't know if your gunner had talked you out of it. I never heard of a snake made of chickenshit, but there's a first time for everything."

I heard my boss laughing from the cockpit.

"You—you tell her to get fucked," I sputtered.

"Ha. I'm not telling her anything of the sort, Snake. Just sit down in the turret and take it, asshole. Serves you right."

"I'm transmitting the nav data to you now, so even your dumb ass won't have an excuse to get lost," she said. The laughing in the cockpit went quiet.

"Hey, I didn't sign on to get insulted," he snapped to Carla over the comm channel.

"No, you signed on for fifteen grand," she radioed back. "And that buys me a whole lot of insults. I'll call you whatever I damn well please."

"Still think she's into you?" I asked the boss.

"Shut up, Snake. That's just foreplay."

"Sweet Jesus, you've got it bad," I said.

"How about you just keep your eyes peeled and your trigger finger warmed up, okay?"

I heard the *beep* from the ship's computer which announced an incoming message and several taps on the boss's keyboard as he sorted through it.

"I don't like this," he radioed Carla, wariness creeping into his voice.

"What's it say? What's going on?" I asked. When I got no response, I climbed out of the turret and made my way forward, poking my head through the hatch into the cramped cockpit so I could read the navigation data over the boss's shoulder.

"Jesus, we've been through this, haven't we?" Carla came back, exasperation in her voice. "I'm on a tight timeline, so I need you to shit or get off the pot. I don't have time for you to whine about how dangerous everything is each step of the way. Just shut up, come with me, make the run, and get fifteen grand, or get lost. Once this is all over, we can hang out and go over the best way to do it in the future, all right? But not until then."

I noticed my boss sat up a little straighter in his seat when she said 'hang out'.

"Talk is cheap, Boss. She's playing you. I looked at the navigation data. Pretty suspicious we don't pick up 'cargo' until Markins, but she's still having us fly through Tellison to get there, don't you think? And she's having us fly the same route back out, too? *Right*. What was shipment's final destination again? Somewhere in Lassiter's Junction? There's a dozen other ways to get to Markins and then to Lassiter's Junction without doing the run through Tellison."

"Oh yeah?" he asked. "And they'd take two and a half months, too. Doing the run to Markins through Tellison only takes three days."

"Did you hear me?" Carla asked over the radio. "You doing this or not? 'Cause if you are, we got to hit the jump to Bascia before twenty-one hundred. I got a source says the insys boys are gonna start doing random boarding inspections and I don't have time to get caught up in all that."

"No. No, no, *no*," I said, shaking my head.

"Snake, c'mon," the boss pleaded.

"You got five seconds to be in or out. *Five, four, three…*" Carla counted.

"I said we were in, and we're in," he said over the radio avoiding eye contact with me. "Let's go."

I sighed and walked back to the ship's mid-quarters where I plopped down onto the sole couch that was our ship's sleeping area. From there, I could make out my boss's back in the cockpit. I gave him a defiant middle finger.

"I'm going to sleep," I announced. "Wake me up when we reach Bascia. From there it's only two hours to the Tellison jump point and I wanna have plenty of time to make my peace with the Creator before you jump us to our deaths." I stretched out on the couch and closed my eyes.

The boss snorted. "Motherfucker, it's gonna take a lot longer than two hours for you to clear accounts with the cosmos. Hell, it would take more than two hours to settle things with *me*."

I opened my eyes and picked my head up off the couch to answer. "Oh, no. Don't start that crap, Boss. After *this* bullshit? We're even."

CHAPTER FIVE

Ten hours later, I sat in the turret nervously scanning the emptiness which was the Tellison system. In the two hours we'd been in Tellison so far, the pirates I feared had not leapt out from wherever they lurked to ambush us, but as I saw it, the risk grew greater with every hour that separated us from the jump point. Carla's menacing Razor flew in tight formation with our Black Sun, below us and at our five o'clock. She'd cut her running lights as soon as we'd entered Tellison, which meant between her ship's flat black finish, our lack of a radar, and the Razor's heat dissipating technologies, she was all but invisible—a ghostly predator in the dark.

Even though it's a major breach of etiquette for a merchant vessel under guard to point its guns at its own escort, I made a show of sweeping across the Razor when I did my scans. She may have charmed my lovelorn boss with her feminine wiles, but I didn't trust her one bit.

"We just cleared nav point five," the boss announced. "Three more hours to marker six, and then from there another fifteen to the Markins jump point. Piece of cake."

"Uh huh, sure," I said. "Let's see if you're still singing the same tune when we reach the jump to Markins. If you're saying anything at all."

An unfamiliar chime accompanied a message on my leftmost VDU: *Point to point laser communications transmission incoming. Open channel?*

The boss must have accepted the offer, because the message disappeared.

Carla's voice over the ship-to-ship laser channel came through faint and garbled. "Use this channel for comms between us until I say different from here on out. If there's anybody out there, they'll be listening for broadcast transmissions."

"Roger," the boss replied. "Will do. Listen, Carla, play it straight. Obviously, you know something's coming, so just level with us and tell us what we're up against."

"You'll know what you need to know when you need to know it," she replied. "Out."

In the turret, the general sense of unease I'd been able to joke about was gone, replaced by a very real sense of dread.

"I'm telling you, Boss," I said, "she's setting us up. She's brought us out here to get killed."

"What sense does that make?" he answered, "She's got no reason to lure us all the way out here with an empty hold. I agree, there's something up, but she's not trying to kill us. If she'd wanted to, she could have done it at the linkup point and saved us all the trip out here. Try again, Snake."

I scowled. He had a good point, but it did nothing to put my mind at ease.

We traveled on in silence across the darkened face of the Tellison Nebula for another forty minutes before he spoke up again.

"Snake, do me a favor. Go to the comms computer and broaden scan range to include restricted-band encrypted channels."

"You want to listen to UNF channels?" I asked as I climbed halfway out of the turret and opened the starboard computer cabinet. "There's not gonna be any UNF out here, and if there are, we wouldn't be able to crack their encryption anyway."

"Yeah, I know," the boss said. "But here's the thing. I just saw a spike on a freq that matches one of their bands. The spike was strong, so the source is close. It may very well be encrypted, but I don't think it's UNF."

I got an icy feeling in my stomach. "From Carla's Razor?"

"Maybe."

"Shit, shit, *shit*," I muttered as I typed in the new scan parameters. Once finished, I dropped back down in the turret and slewed my guns over to cover Carla.

Just what kind of game was Carla playing?

A message from our encryption software popped up on one of my screens: *beginning real-time comms decryption*.

"You seeing the message about the encryption, Boss?" I asked.

"Yep. I see it."

The decryption software cut us into the middle of a conversation.

" —out of luck," said a sneering male voice. "We know when the runs are scheduled, bitch. We know what you got. You tell your merchie friend to dump it right now, then you two hightail it out of here, and we might let you go. You make us work for it, and you're gonna regret it."

"Negative," Carla said. "Listen, you fucks. Where's Anders? You tell that shithead he's already been paid once, and my employers aren't gonna pay twice."

"What the fuck is she talking about?" the boss shouted from the cockpit. "We've got an empty hold. There's nothing to dump!"

The sneering man's reply to Carla cut me off before I could answer. "You wanna talk to Anders? Who do you think you are, the goddamn UNF general secretary? Anders only talks to clients, bitch, and that ain't you."

I slewed my turret around, looking for whoever Carla was talking too. I nearly jumped out of my skin.

On our port side, emerging from the distant darkness of the Tellison nebula, was a massive Scania-Peterbilt Galaxy Runner, probably originally a colony ship but long since modified for other, less pleasant tasks. I zoomed in with my gun camera just in time to see a pair of fighters drop out the bottom, angled right for us.

"Boss! We got contacts, port side! Big Peterbilt and two fighters. Range is—" Instinctively, I looked down at my radar display to give him a range. The screen was blank. "Fuck! Range is—"

"I know," he called back. "Range is 'I broke the array.' I got it. You're gonna have to keep me informed, 'cause I can't see them from the cockpit and without radar, I got no way of telling where they are."

"Should we tell Carla?" I asked.

"I'm pretty sure she already knows," he said grimly.

I watched in horror as four more fighters emerged from the hulking vessel.

"We're coming for you, cunt," a different harsh voice said over the encrypted channel. "He dumps that cargo, or you got about five minutes 'till we open your merchie friend up and see what he's made of, and you along with him."

"Boss, they just launched four more fighters. He's not kidding. Fuck this job," I said. "It's time to run."

"Where to?" the boss asked weakly. "Even maxed out, we can't run from those fighters—and sure as hell not three hours back to the jump point. Our only chance is to stick with Carla long enough for her to buy us some time. I'm just hoping she sticks with us."

Fuck.

He was right, but it was not a reassuring thought.

"Three minutes," the harsh voice warned again.

"Like I said," Carla shot back, apparently unconcerned, "I want to talk to Anders. I got a right."

"Bitch, you got no rights except what we give you."

"Fine," Carla answered over the encrypted channel. "But when you tell Anders you jumped Maria Vega escorting a load for Mr. Tanaka, you let me know how that works out for you."

The response was laughter. "You got a sense of humor. Maria Vega is dead. Roscoe stamped her in Pinewood two weeks ago."

"Really? That what Roscoe said? 'Cause here I am. Come to think of it, when's the last time you heard from Roscoe? About a week ago, maybe?" Carla taunted.

"What are you talkin' about?" There was a note of doubt in the man's voice.

"Tell you what. I'm gonna send you a picture of Roscoe—what's left of him. You see it gets to Anders, and tell him next time he should send a pro to do it instead of his son."

The computer *beeped*, but messages don't display at my station. I didn't need to see it, because the boss's reaction told me all I needed to know. "Holy fuck, they must have hit him with a laz rifle."

A new voice came across the encrypted channel, enraged and bitter. "You fucking cunt, Vega! I will cut you to pieces and drink your fucking blood! I'm coming for you!"

"I'd hoped you were out there, Anders," Carla said in a tone of voice that told me she was grinning from ear to ear. "I'm coming for you too."

In the distance, a bright yellow glow silhouetted the incoming fighters—afterburners.

"Boss, they didn't like that very much. They're coming in quick."

"Black Sun, you got multiple contacts off the port side," Carla told us, this time on the regular broadcast channel. "They are hostile. I'm engaging."

"Yeah, no shit, Carla," the boss radioed back. "We aren't as dumb as you take us for. We've been listening to your little chit chat. You got some explaining to do."

"Maybe later," Carla said as her Razor rolled underneath us and her afterburners kicked on, headed straight at the Peterbilt and its complement of fighters.

"Snake, we gotta close with her," the boss said as the ship heeled around to face the incoming fighters. "They probably won't be able to get a good lock on the Razor, but they aren't gonna have that problem with us. Only way to survive is to stick within gun range."

I grunted. He was right, but the problem with sticking inside gun range was we were a pretty big target compared to Carla, and they had a whole hell of a lot more guns than we did.

The ship shuddered as the boss engaged our afterburners to close the distance between us and the fighters.

"Shit! Snake, they got a lock!"

"I'm on it," I shouted, scanning through targeting frequencies with my left hand while keeping the guns facing the nearest fighter with my right. When I saw the tell-tale waveform that marked a missile's targeting radar on my left VDU, I highlighted it and pressed the worn "active countermeasure" button.

The boss rolled the ship left and I heard the muffled *whump* of our chaff dispenser kicking out thousands of radar-attracting pieces of foil. Space lit up somewhere to our right.

"I think we just dodged one," I told the boss as I continued to scan, even though years of practice kept diverting my attention to the blank radar screen.

"Yeah," he said, "but there'll be more for sure—fuck!" The ship jerked right and then dove.

I couldn't see whatever had spooked the boss, but that was fine by me. I had plenty to worry about as it was-a yellow Banshee fighter coming at us from forward and low, filling space with laser fire. I couldn't get a range to him, but I figured if he was shooting at me, I was close enough to shoot back.

Keeping up the scan-identify-jam pattern to keep the missiles at bay with my left hand, I trained my guns on the small fighter and sent a burst right back at the Banshee. His shields flared as my rounds hit, but he pulled up and out of my sight.

"Got one diving on you," Carla radioed. In the background, there was the unmistakable sound of a missile lock warning.

The boss rolled the ship on its x axis, bringing a diving Puma 120 into my cone of fire. His shots took our bottom shields down to what my readout said was twenty-five percent, but the extended burst I put into his forward shields collapsed them completely. As the Puma afterburned away from us, I saw debris trailing behind him.

"You'll think twice about that shit again, won't you motherfucker?" I muttered.

"Got one on you, Carla, six o'clock high," the boss radioed.

"Roger," Carla replied. "Watch out for that—" Whatever she said next was drowned out by the loud screech of an alarm going off in her cockpit.

"I got it," the boss said and pulled the ship into a climb. "Port side, low. He's—"

"Watch out!" Carla interrupted. "Imrec away— don't—*shit*."

I cut the comms off in the turret.

"Boss, I cut comms," I shouted. "Anything important, let me know."

"Yep. You got a visual on anything?"

"Two too far out to hit, but for all I know somebody's creeping up our ass from six high. I can't see and without radar it's pretty tough down here, you know?" I asked.

"You should try flying without it, it's almost impossible to—" A vibrant, glowing blue line appeared below the ship, close enough to bathe the turret in pale blue light for half an instant. "Fuck! Railguns, Snake."

"Yeah," I said, wiping a sweaty palm on my pant leg. "I saw it. That shit about picked me off the bottom of this rustbucket."

He didn't reply. Instead, he jerked the ship hard to the left as another blue line appeared in space beneath us. A silver FRL99 streaked between us and the light, tailed by Carla's Razor, guns blazing.

As I slewed the turret further left to clear a firing Delta off Carla's tail, I caught the explosion that marked the end of the FRL out of the corner of my eye.

"She got one, Boss!" I called.

The ship shook from repeated hits and I heard a series of warning alarms go off overhead. The boss dove hard, which gave me a beautiful topshot on the Puma I'd damaged earlier. My first burst shredded his shields and the second punched through his armor. The fighter exploded in a ball of fire and sent flaming wreckage in every direction.

"And scratch one for me!" I shouted.

I didn't have time to pat myself on the back, though. I worked through two more jamming cycles while I found another target, a different Delta than the one I'd seen trailing Carla before, this one painted yellow and black and sporting three lasers forward. I fired at him, but he cut his throttles and passed underneath the ship to a position somewhere behind us. The ship shook violently, and the boss swore.

We climbed again and the massive Peterbilt loomed into view, with Carla's black Razor in silhouette as she fired a pair of missiles at a distant target. Even though I doubted I'd scratch their shields, I fired a long burst at the Peterbilt, receiving a barrage of orange laser fire in return.

"Snake, whatever you just did, how 'bout cutting it out, 'kay?" the boss called as he maneuvered us through the dancing beams.

Our Black Sun 490 dove and the boss rolled us right, avoiding yet another shot from the Peterbilt's railguns but bringing us perilously close to a purple blur that blazed past me so fast I couldn't even tell what kind of fighter it was. As a flash of yellow on my left caught my eye and as I spun the turret to try to get a shot on the Delta, our impact warning alarm blared. Carla's Razor appeared out of the dark, so close I could actually see warning lights going off in her cockpit. I saw her helmeted head snap up at me and then she was gone, slipping underneath us and forward.

My heart hammered in my chest. "Jesus *fuck*, she almost hit us!" I shouted.

Apparently, Carla wasn't thrilled either, as I heard the boss shouting back.

"Fuck no, I can't see you. Snake told you our targeting system was down."

I couldn't hear her response, but I did hear his.

"Of course, he was serious!"

The ship shuddered and there was an instant of quiet as the onboard lights and circulation flickered off and back on again. I risked a nervous look upward just to make sure nothing overhead was on fire.

"Yo, Snake," my boss called, voice high-pitched and nervous. "Port side shield generator's overloaded, and if it goes, we're gonna lose life support too. I'm gonna have to shut it down and bleed the capacitor before I restart it. Don't let us get shot from port, all right?"

"Shit. No promises."

"I figured," he muttered.

He turned to put our starboard side toward the Peterbilt, hoping, I guess, that all the enemy fighters would politely stay between it and us while we completed the restart. The problem with that approach became very obvious, very quickly—the purple blur I had seen earlier was, in fact, an Indus F. He paralleled our course for a second, pulled into a high loop and came at us, twin lasers on the rampage.

From the port side.

The ship shuddered from repeated hits and a loud *scree* from above told me we'd lost pressure in the cargo hold. The ship's computer intoned "*fire, fire, fire,*" followed by the *whoosh* of an automatic fire bottle. I fired back, throwing off the Indus's aim, but the pilot pulled up and disappeared.

"Roll to starboard!" I shouted.

"But the Peterbilt!" the boss yelled, even as he rolled hard to starboard like I'd asked. In addition, the boss threw on the thrust reversers, decelerating us so quickly I almost slammed into my gun status VDU.

The sudden move brought the Indus back into my field of fire. My shots lanced into him, disappearing into showers of sparks as they impacted his shields. The Indus broke off his attack run and hit his afterburners and he passed forward of our Black Sun 490.

And right into Carla's gunfire.

I had just enough time to see the pilot's ejection seat blast clear of the wreckage before the boss put the ship into a sudden dive and rolled back to port. We passed through a burst of orange fire from the Peterbilt which took our shields down to virtually nothing before drawing the attention of the yellow and black Delta I'd been trying to hit earlier.

He strafed us topside, and the boss muttered something about our top-mounted sensor package. The boss hit the afterburner and rolled while I scanned, trying to find the Delta, but the pilot was no amateur. He matched us, corkscrew for turn, keeping just out of my sight and putting out some serious fire.

"Snake, give this guy a nosebleed, would you?"

"Working on it. But he's just—*damn it*—he's good."

"He's got a lock on us, Snake!" the boss shouted.

I scanned through the missile frequencies as fast as I could. From our ship, I saw a trail of flares punching out into the dark along with two new clouds of chaff. I heard a sigh of relief from the boss and guessed we'd beaten the missile lock.

The relief was short lived.

A railgun shot passed close behind and orange lasers reached out for us, scoring a few hits against our already weakened forward shields. One laser got through and melted a deep hole in the armor not a meter from the turret. I tried to keep calm by reminding myself the clear polymer that made up my turret was rated to take a direct hit from a J class laser—and tried to forget that a manufacturer will tell you anything you'll believe as long it makes you buy whatever the hell it is they're trying to sell you.

Behind us, the Delta started firing again, and again we went back into our spinning corkscrew dance. The boss shouted something over the radio to Carla, but couldn't make it out over the sound of various alarms and my own heart pounding as I tried to draw a bead on the Delta.

Carla scissored across my vision, trailed by a Super Storm. I risked pulling off the Delta long enough to penetrate his shields and scorch his armor before I lost him.

Shit.

I slewed the turret in a vain attempt to follow the Delta and noted, much to my horror, that the Peterbilt was dead ahead and closing fast. Orange laser fire and blue railgun shots lit the space around us as the boss juked along every axis to throw off their gunners' aim.

"What the fuck are you doing, Bossman?" I asked.

"Making a run for the nebula while we still can."

"The nebula? We go in there without a targeting radar and we'll be lucky we don't find an asteroid the hard way." I didn't like this plan one bit and liked it even less when the next thought struck me: "Shit, man, without the radar will we even be able to find our way back out again?"

"We've still got navigation, Snake, but, yeah, a radar would be a big help. And while we *might* die in there, we're definitely gonna bite it if we stay out here!"

More shots buffeted the ship, and loud *bang* from engine three told me we had compressor damage.

By now, the Peterbilt was close enough for me to line up good shots, so I figured I might as well go down swinging. I poured fire into him, but his shields had no trouble stopping my lasers.

There was an incredulous "*What?*" from the boss, followed by a long string of curses.

"What is it?" I asked, bracing for the worst.

"Carla's got a torpedo—military issue. A real carrier killer. She's lining up for a shot on the Peterbilt."

"So, what the hell's she been waiting for, then?"

"She said something about electronic counter-countermeasures and phased shielding frequencies. How the fuck should I know, Snake? All I know is she said she's taking the shot."

By now the massive gray Peterbilt filled the view in front of us, obscured only by the mass of orange laser fire. An impact warning sounded and the boss pulled up sharply. The Delta who'd been trailing us the entire time chose to dive under his mothership instead, and I shifted my futile fire off the Peterbilt and onto the yellow and black fighter. His shields arced and glowed.

Just before he disappeared underneath the Peterbilt, I saw a jet of flame spurt from his left wing.

The massive ship flashed under us, topside turrets reaching at us the whole time and scoring several more hits. Sparks showered from the computer cabinet above the turret, sending stinging hot bits into the turret with me, but I couldn't afford to care. I had my hands full trying to break a dozen missile locks from the hulking pirate carrier. A solid burst from one of the turrets hit us in the rear quarter. Our internal lights winked out again, replaced by red emergency lighting. The radiation alarm buzzed.

Space went pitch black as we punched into the inky darkness of the Tellison Nebula.

We flew on for another tense moment but the Delta who had been pursuing us didn't seem to want to follow us into the nebula. The boss killed the number three engine and silenced the ship's various alarms. The ship slowed and he rolled it over nose to tail so we'd be facing out the exact way we'd come in. We slowed to a halt and I heard furious typing from the cockpit as the boss toggled through various menus, assessing the damage.

I looked down at the puddle of sweat in the turret and pried my white knuckles off the gun controls. I kept cycling through frequencies with my left, just in case, even though a missile lock in the nebula was a remote possibility.

I flipped the comms at my station back on just in time to hear Carla taunting us.

"Where'd you go, amigos? You're gonna miss the show." Over her transmission I heard her ship's computer intone *"Firing solution complete. Hit probability ninety-nine point nine percent. Fire at will."*

"Oh, we wouldn't want to miss that," the boss replied, voice dripping sarcasm. "We'll sit tight, thanks. I dunno if you remember how you sold me on this job, but you hired a cargo ship, not a fucking missile frigate. Between the Delta and that damn pirate carrier Peterbilt and the damage we've already taken, we're not coming out till he's dead or you are."

"The Delta is dead," Carla said. "Snake got him. Pretty good shooting."

"Don't even open your damn mouth, Snake," the boss warned. "I'm not in the mood."

I shrugged.

"Whatcha thinking?" the boss asked me.

"I think we'd better be damn careful. She's obviously a smooth operator and a dangerous pilot, but I'm not sure I buy she's got a torp. I think she's just trying to get us to come back out for bait so she can either get away or hit him with missiles."

"And now the Peterbilt is dead too, and Anders along with it," Carla radioed triumphantly.

The boss snorted. "Listen to her all happy, Snake. You know what? Even if she did kill it, what's to say she doesn't just wipe us out and not pay us?" he mused.

"Yeah, because if—"

Ahead, the blackness evaporated, replaced by a wall of pure blinding white light, stripping the black dust of the nebula away in an eyeblink. I closed my eyes to shield my seared retinas and my hands came up to shield my face involuntarily.

Through my closed eyelids, I could make out the bones in my fingers.

The light dissipated and I opened my eyes. My vision was full of spots and the image of my skeletal fingers lingered. As best I could tell we were still alive, but the part of the nebula's dust cloud we'd been using for concealment was no more—along with the pirate flagship. I had a sudden metallic taste in my mouth, which made no sense until every radiation alarm in the ship started chirping rad spike warnings.

"Snake," the boss coughed. "You still alive down there?"

"Yeah, I think so," I said as my vision blurred. "But I got a pretty good radiation dose. Like, a lot. I don't feel so good."

"That's what I was afraid of, buddy," he said.

I tried to climb out of the turret but collapsed back into my seat. I heard his flight harness unbuckle and then a storage locker open. I closed my eyes and was treated again to the psychedelic vision of my finger bones. My tongue tasted like steel and I felt like I was going to be sick.

The boss appeared above me in the turret hatch, worry etched across his face. He tossed down a pair of autoinjectors which landed on my chest.

"Use those," he said. "And after that, I've got the exposure pills."

I nodded weakly, fumbled around getting the cap off the first one, and pressed it to my right thigh. The needle hurt, but my nausea subsided almost instantly. I flipped the safety cap off the second injector and hit myself in the left thigh. A coolness washed over me, and the metallic taste began to fade. I pulled up the autoinjectors and looked at the label. I frowned.

"Boss," I rasped, "these things expired two years ago."

He shrugged. "I'm sure they still work. They just put expiration dates on there to get you to buy new ones, you know?"

"Yeah, sure, whatever. How old are the exposure pills?"

He checked the box. "Umm, good news there, Snake. They only expired last month."

I shrugged. "I'll take what I can get, I guess."

He tossed the box down along with a bottle of water.

CHAPTER SIX

Four hours later, the boss and I stood amidships, lit by red emergency lighting. We wore our full environmental protection suits except our helmets, which we'd just removed after getting back in from our walk around our unpressurized cargo bay to check for damage.

"I counted three breaches. How about you?" the boss asked me.

"Yeah. And the one by the port hydraulic reservoir is gonna be a bitch to patch," I answered.

"Aww, shit. I didn't even think about that, because of the—"

"Yeah."

"Did it puncture the tank too?"

I snorted. "Of course. I think it may have caught the line on fire too, but I couldn't tell for sure."

The boss frowned. "That would explain why we've got oxygen generation, but CO_2 scrubbing is at fifty percent. The portside filter bank probably burned up with it. Also means we probably lost all our port side sensors from the midships back. The lines run through the same conduit."

"Shit," I said with a glance at my notebook. "I'll add it to the list."

I sighed. It had been four hours since the boss and I had started our damage assessment, and we still hadn't figured out everything wrong with our Black Sun 490. We hadn't had functioning comms of any sort since the radiation spike from the Peterbilt's reactor going critical. Instead, we'd been reduced to sending Carla Morse code messages via emergency flashlight, since we didn't even have running lights or interior lighting. Only the number one engine was operational. Primary navigation was out, but the boss thought it would come back on with a reboot of the ship's main computer, although he didn't want to try *that* for fear that with all the sensors we had damaged, the computer would freeze in diagnostic mode on restart. Judging by the radiation damage, our radiation shields were shot, and Carla had confirmed with us via Morse code that all our reentry heat shields had been holed through with laser fire. According to the ship's computer, our top-mounted planetary navigation and weather suite wasn't responding, which we felt pretty sure was because it wasn't there anymore. In addition, despite the boss's best efforts, there had been a capacitor fire in bank five, which meant the port side shield generator was probably a solid piece of fused metal. The jump drive was still functional, although we were showing power fluctuations indicating a slight variation in the core temperature.

The final indignity was that our toilet no longer flushed, which meant the blood-filled piss I'd taken after the anti-radiation shots had done their work was still in the bowl, probably irradiating the tiny latrine.

The boss climbed back into the cockpit and flipped a few switches. He muttered something under his breath, punched a button, and slapped the side of one of his VDUs.

"Okay, here goes, Snake." He flipped another switch and the ship's interior lighting came back on.

"Hey," I said with a grin. "It's back."

The lighting died and the red emergency lighting flickered back to life.

"I swear to fucking God, *something* better start working around here or I am going to lose my mind," he mumbled.

"What now?"

"Now I'm gonna try comms again," he said. He ran through some menus, flipped a switch, and hit a button on his keyboard. "Shit. Oh, wait a minute—*that's* why. Snake, check and see if circuit breaker thirty-one is tripped in the midships box."

I opened the breaker box and flipped number thirty-one to *on*.

"Try it now," I called.

He pressed a key and was rewarded with a *beep* from the console.

"Yes! We're back up. We don't have radio comms, but it looks like we still should have point to point laser comms. I'll hail Carla and see."

"You do that, Boss, and tell her she's got a whole lot of explaining to do."

"Carla, can you read us?"

"I read you. You two still alive in there?" Her mocking tone did not sit well with me.

"Listen, you lying, crazy bitch," the boss snarled. Apparently, her tone didn't sit well with him either. "We are still alive and you'd better be glad, because if we'd died, I was gonna come back and haunt your every dream!"

"Calm down, I'll explain when we reach Bascia Station—"

"Bascia?" the boss cut in. "I thought the job was a run to Markins?"

"Follow me to Bascia Station," she repeated. "Carla, out."

"Come on," I said from my position on the couch. "You still think there's any truth to whatever bullshit she told you back at the bar? Besides, we can't even land on Markins anyway. No heat shields for reentry, remember? I say if she wants to end it early rather than fly through the rest of Tellison, let's go for it."

The boss looked over his shoulder at me. "I'm worried about the paycheck. After this mess, we're going to need all the cash we can get. Last thing I want to do is land and have her say we didn't execute the contract."

"I know you got a lot of funny ideas about chivalry," I said. "But she's a bounty hunter, plain and simple. And in the world she runs in, there ain't no guys or girls—you're either a killer or a body. I suggest you start looking at her the same way. If she tries to back out of paying, I think staring her down the barrel of that pistol you wear would go a long way toward changing her mind."

The boss turned around and slouched lower in his seat. I'd seen that posture from him before, although it was usually in a booth. He didn't have to say anything for me to know what he was thinking: *I guess I'm not gonna get laid tonight, either*.

I dropped back down in the turret and began cycling through the ship systems, checking for any damage that had escaped our notice. I figured the long, slow trip back to the jump point on one engine would give me plenty of time to find anything we missed.

Unfortunately, while the boss and I break a lot of laws, the one law that *never* gets broken belongs to Murphy.

Not five minutes after I'd gotten comfortable, Carla's voice piped back up over the comm set.

"Hey, ace, you got a large heat bloom coming off your number one engine."

The boss tapped on his keyboard a few times before he answered. "I'm not showing any—"

The explosion and rush of air and heat startled me so much that had I not already taken my post-radiation-poisoning piss I probably would have wet myself. As it was, I looked up from the turret just in time to see a fireball flame into the crew cabin just above the turret ring. It died as quickly as it had come, but when it did, so did everything else. I waited for the emergency lighting and life support to come back on, but they—like most of the rest of the ship, it seemed—had given up.

The ship was as silent as a grave.

"Boss, you all right up there?" I called into the darkness.

"Yeah, I think so. My ears are ringing like a sonofabitch, though."

I smiled. "It'll get better in a day or two. That's what they told me at the aid station after you almost shot my head off a few days ago anyway."

"I appreciate your concern," he muttered.

"What happened?"

"Fuck if I know," he said. "I wasn't showing anything abnormal on the readings. Probably got a coolant leak but the sensor that's supposed to tell us and the engine got shot up, so the system ran to failure."

"Any chance the reactor went critical?"

"If it did, we wouldn't still be here."

I sighed in the dark. "Okay. What now?"

"Well, *now*, I try to restart, which probably won't work. After that, we put on our EVP helmets back on." I heard the boss shuffling around in the cockpit, then open a computer cabinet.

"And wait? For what, the next passing pirate crew or salvage team to come by and jack our lifeless corpses?" I asked.

"Nope. We'll go outside, have an external look at the damage and see if we can reset the engines from the maintenance access out there."

"You are out of your mind," I argued. "You want to vent what little air and heat we have left out, so we can get outside in an EVP suit rated for three hours to attempt a fix I can already tell you isn't going to work? I'd rather just shoot myself, thanks."

"Look," he said, exasperated. "What else can we do?"

"Ask Carla for help."

"Fuck that bitch. She's the one who got us into this mess. Weren't you just saying to her everybody's a killer or a body? Why would she help us when it would be easier just to let us die out here?"

"Well, I did say that, yeah," I conceded. "But that was before we needed her help. *Now*, I say let's take a chance on her humanity and generosity."

Harsh light streamed in through the cockpit. I poked my head up from the turret into the blinding glare of Carla's searchlights. They flicked on and off in rapid succession and I struggled to decode the message as fast as she sent it. It took a second, but I finally got it.

Hope you have EVP suits onboard. Sit tight. Called for jump tug.

"No," the boss said. "Absolutely not. I've never been towed and I'm not starting now. The fee will kill us."

Using his flashlight, he flicked back his message: *No need for tug. We'll be fine.*

Behind him, using my cigarette lighter as the light and my hand to signal, I sent back my own reply, which he couldn't read: *No, we won't. He's an idiot. Call tug.*

Her reply came back in the same rapid-fire pace she'd used before: *Too late, ace. Knew you wouldn't make it. Called tug 5 hours ago. ETA 45 mins.*

"God *damn* it, do I hate this girl," the boss muttered.

Carla killed her searchlights and turned on her cockpit illumination instead. She'd taken her helmet off and her Razor hung close enough for us to barely make out her face. She smirked and shook her head at us. Just before her cockpit lights blinked out, I thought I saw her wink. I wasn't sure until I heard the boss's dumbfounded voice in the darkness.

"Did she just wink at me?"

I smiled.

That's one possibility.

───────────────────────

We sat glumly in the passenger area of the *Retriever's Star*; the jump tug Carla had summoned for us. As if being a passenger aboard someone else's ship wasn't bad enough, we had a wonderful view of our battered ship through the starboard windows suspended in the tug's recovery apparatus. From the exterior, the damage looked even worse than it did on the inside: slag marks pockmarked the entire ship, and a long string of scorch marks ran along its spine. From outside, it was obvious the number one engine was a total loss, as was the ECM suite, which had been bolted in its mount atop the engine. The only good news was that Carla's Razor, running lights on, was visible through the port side windows. She hadn't left us without paying just yet.

I sat wrapped in a blanket to help me recover from the chill I'd gotten waiting for the tug to arrive and take us aboard and sipped a mug of black coffee while wishing for something stronger. Beside me, the boss sulked and stared into his own cup.

The hatch from the crew cabin swung open to admit one of the ship's crew into the passenger cabin.

The older man looked like he'd been around the block a few dozen times, his face and fingers scarred. He crossed his arms in front of him before he spoke, and I noticed his right hand rested on the butt of the pistol he kept in his shoulder holster.

"Now, about payment," he said with a raised eyebrow. "I don't get very many calls to Tellison, for pretty obvious reasons, but I ain't asking questions about what you two fools were doing out there, just like I didn't ask your lady friend. Her credit was good, so I came. But that was to get me out here. Now let's talk about what it's gonna take to get you back."

The boss looked up and I saw his eyes flash to the man's pistol.

"Okay, let's talk rates," the boss said with a sigh. He made a show of spreading his arms wide and rested them nonchalantly on the adjacent seats. His pistol was far out of reach. The man visibly relaxed.

"It's twenty-five hundred for me to leave the yard," the old man said. "And a grand per jump. And an extra five hundred to go to Tellison—hazard pay. Plus fifteen hundred for the elevator."

"Elevator?" the boss asked incredulously. "Where are you coming from? The nearest planet with a space elevator is Greenly."

"Sounds like you just answered your own question," the man said.

"Well, we don't need to go all the way back there," I said. "Just drop us off at Bascia Station."

"Yeah," the boss agreed. "Or Rucker Watson's, since you gotta go back through the N25 jump point to get to Greenly anyway."

The tug operator laughed. "I can tell you boys don't know how this business works. Stations don't take ships too damaged to dock under their own power, so Bascia and RW's are out, which means you have to go back somewhere with an elevator or an orbital complex, and I'll be damned if we're going all the way to Diis. Plus, I'm the one with your ship in my docking collars, which means I'll take you where I damn well choose."

He had a point. The boss and I shared a resigned look.

"Fine," the boss said. "So, it's what? Let's see: two and a half grand for the tow, one apiece for two jumps, five hundred for coming to Tellison, and one and a half grand for the space elevator? So that's… six and a half grand?"

"Plus tax," the man said.

"Fine. Plus tax," the boss agreed through gritted teeth.

"Plus the other two thousand."

"*Other* two thousand? For what?" I asked incredulously.

"I had to jump out here to get you, didn't I? You gotta pay for jumps both ways."

My eyes narrowed. "Bullshit. It's gonna take us a day to get to Greenly at the least, but you got here in like six hours. You couldn't have been any further out than Bascia when she called."

"He's right," the boss said. "Where were you when she called? The T53 outpost out there at junction two? Marker nine? We're not paying for the jumps some other sucker already paid you for."

"I don't know what you're talking about," the man said with a smile. "All I know is, you can calculate your rate your way and I'll calculate it mine and we'll see which one gets your ship released. You got a day to think about it." He stepped back through the hatch and closed it behind him.

"And *that* is why I didn't want to get towed," the boss said.

"Would you rather be dead?"

"Doesn't matter. We might as well be. I've only got five and a half in the account."

"Carla owes us fifteen large, boss. Call her and tell her to transfer the money."

"I just hate having to use the money we just made for a job just to get back—"

"What difference does it make?" I asked. "Call her and get the money."

"Oh, I'm gonna call her, all right. I'ma call her and tell her the next time she fucks me like this, it goddamn better be in a bed, that's what I'm gonna do," he groused as he stared back into his mug.

"Well, *that* sure isn't gonna get us anywhere. You want me to call her?"

The boss looked up at me in surprise. "Ha. She doesn't even talk to you. I'll call her. Besides, she winked at me, remember?"

Denial springs eternal.

Something must have shown on my face because the boss's eyes narrowed. "*Wait a minute.*

You think she winked at… *you?* That *is* what you think. I can see it in your eyes."

I plopped down in the seat across from him. "You want to know what I think? What I *really* think?"

"Go ahead. Enlighten me."

"I don't think that wink was meant for you, no. Well, not exactly."

"What's that supposed to mean?"

"I think she's just fucking with you by trying to make you pissed off at me," I said. And to be honest, that's what I actually thought. Mostly.

"So, you think she's just trying to get under my skin?" he asked. "What for?"

"Why do *you* think?" I responded.

"Because she kinda likes me, but she's afraid to let it show."

I laughed. "Oh, you think so? She's like twenty-five, not fifteen, boss. This isn't fuckin' high school."

"Fine. So, answer my damn question. Why do *you* think she's trying to get under my skin?" he snapped.

"Simple. She doesn't like you, so seeing you pissed off makes her happy."

The boss gave me the middle finger. "Fuck you, Snake. Sit tight while I call her about the money."

He stood and walked the length of the cabin to knock on the hatch. It cracked open a bit and a middle-aged woman poked her head out.

"Yes?"

"Can I use your comms to call our partner on this job? She's gonna have to transfer some money so we can... Well, anyway, we just need... the money."

As the boss choked out his last few words, I covered my smirk with my hand. I'd always found it funny how much he hated to admit when he was out of money or needed help, even though he should have been used to it by this point in his life.

"Oh, you can't make the payment, huh, sweetie? Well, I hope she loans it to you—"

"No, we can make the payment," the boss protested. "And it's not a loan, it's what she owes—"

The woman ignored him and kept talking. "I'm sorry, but you can't use our comms. Company policy. You know what channel she's running on? There's a pay station over there, honey." She pointed a hand through the hatch to the back wall, toward a dull gray meter-by-meter cube with a scuffed screen attached.

The woman closed the hatch, leaving the boss fuming, his hands balled into fists.

"The next time I read about one of these tugs getting bushwhacked out past the H115 jump point, I'm gonna laugh my ass off," he declared as he stomped over to the pay station.

CHAPTER SEVEN

———————————————▶

"Oh, it's you again," Carla said by way of hello as she opened the comm channel.

"Yeah, it's me again. Who else would it be?" the boss asked.

"What do you want?"

"We want our money, Carla. You owe us fifteen large and we want it."

Carla chuckled. I noticed she had quite an attractive laugh. "You can't pay the tug fee, can you?" she asked. "Horace hit you with some bullshit jump calculations, did he?"

"Wait. You *know* this guy?" I asked.

"Who's that talking?" Carla said.

"That's Snake," the boss answered.

"Who?"

I scowled. She knew damn well who I was.

"Snake. You know, my turret gunner."

"Oh. Him. I only talk to whoever's in charge, ace. So, tell your pet reptile to get lost."

The boss chortled as my expression darkened. I gave him the finger.

"He's run along, Carla," he told her. "I think you hurt poor Snake's feelings."

"He'll live. So, what's up? You need the money to pay Horace?"

"I didn't say that."

"You didn't have to," she said. "I know Horace well enough to know when he has somebody over a barrel, he squeezes 'em for every credit he can get, but whatever. Send me your payment info and I'll transfer it to you. Fifteen grand, as promised."

He fumbled through a few menus on the touchscreen, typed in the transfer number, and hit send. A dialogue box said *Message Received*.

"Okay, Carla, you got it. But I can't see my account from here. How do I know you'll pay it? I don't wanna walk in to pay Horace or whatever his name is and find out you shorted us."

"Flyboy, if I wanted to get away without paying up, I could'a done it a hundred times already. You're gonna have to trust me on this."

"Ha!" the boss barked. "Last time I trusted you, you led us on some crazy death run. Trust is running mighty damn low at the moment, Carla."

"That's on you, not me."

"Speaking of trust, what was all that bullshit out at the nav point anyway? Just what were you doing out there? What was the real job?" he demanded.

"I'm not talking about it over an open channel, and if you know what's good for you, you won't either. When we get down to Greenly, I'll explain. Pad nine. South spaceport."

"Damn it, Carla, we want some answers and I'm not—"

"Carla out," she said, and closed the channel.

———————————————

The cold rain came down in buckets, soaking me and the boss as we stood outside in the Greenly night. We watched the crane operators move our battle-scarred Black Sun 490 off the space elevator and onto a pad under the harsh spotlights at the west spaceport.

"Shit, man, it hurts the heart," I said.

"Yeah," the boss agreed, eyes never leaving the ship. "I know the feeling, Snake. When you spend as much time aboard as we do, she's like family. Seeing the ship like this is like... like something bad happened to your mom, and you're watching the nurses move her from one bed at the hospital to another. You look at her and wonder if she's in pain. How she feels. It's sad. Like you said, man, 'it hurts the heart.' I know what you mean, for sure."

I gave him an incredulous look. "Obviously you don't know what I mean, because I didn't mean any of *that*. What hurts *my* heart is how much work it's gonna take to get it back flying. I could give two shits how the ship looks. Or how it 'feels.'"

"You know, Snake, only you could somehow make standing out in the pouring rain at night watching other people move my beat-up ship around feel even worse. So, thanks for being there for me, bud."

"Sorry. All your other friends were busy, I guess."

After another hour of maneuver, the crane finally set the ship down. Working as quickly as we could given the wind and rain, the boss and I secured the ship and connected it to the spaceport utility hookups. Then we waited in the rain a half an hour longer until the crew of the *Retriever's Star* showed up so we could authorize the transfer of a whopping eleven thousand, three hundred and ninety-two credits from our account to theirs to cover the recovery, jumps, fees, taxes, and whatever other outright theft they could come up with.

"What now?" I asked when we were back aboard our darkened ship, hoping he would say we were packing our bags for the local shipper's hostel.

"We change out of these wet clothes and then we go to pad nine at the south spaceport and get some answers from Carla," he answered, voice full of resolve and dashing my hopes for sleep anytime soon.

"Tonight?"

"Yes, tonight. She said she'd wait for us, but I don't want to push our luck."

"Boss, she already paid us. Let it go. What more do you think you're gonna get from her?"

"Answers, Snake, like I said. I want to know who she was working for."

"Why? What difference does it make?" I asked, throwing my hands up.

"I dunno," he said. "Maybe I was born curious like you were born an asshole. Or *maybe*, I want to know what the real story is because I want to know if we need to be watching our back, and if so, who from. Maybe that."

I opened my mouth to argue but realized I didn't actually have a come back to his line of logic. I shrugged. "Pad nine it is, I guess."

By the time we got to the south spaceport another hour had passed, but so had the storm. When we got off the tram, the first thing I noticed was the massive apartment buildings that towered over the east side of the spaceport and continued in an unbroken string of lights as far as I could see. The second thing I noticed was how much newer and nicer the south spaceport was than the spaceport where we'd spent the last few miserable hours.

"Wow. Carla keeps her ship in the nice part of town," I said.

"Yeah, and that's why," the boss said as he pointed to a gleaming yellow sign, which read *Long Term and Greenly Resident Storage, Pads 1-75.*

"She lives here, huh?"

"Looks that way."

We followed the signs to pad nine around two huge maintenance buildings to the pads themselves, arranged in rows of ten.

Pad nine wasn't hard to find.

It was the one without a ship parked in it.

The boss and I stared at each other without saying anything for a few seconds, then we cut loose cursing at Carla, kicking gravel, and generally making a scene.

"Excuse me," a voice said from behind us. "You two looking for Carla?"

We turned around to see a uniformed security guard eyeing us warily.

"Actually, yes we are," the boss said. "How'd you know?"

"She told me she had to fly out to a private pad unexpectedly, but two men might come looking for her. She said you'd be upset you didn't find her and probably start acting the fool."

I had to hand it to her—she knew us pretty well for only having worked with us once.

"So glad she gave you such a good description," the boss said sarcastically. "So, what's her info?"

"She wrote it on a piece of paper," he said, digging through his pockets. "Here it is." He pulled out a yellow scrap of folded paper and handed it to the boss.

The boss unfolded it, read it, refolded it, and handed it to me with a deliberate calm that told me he was ready to explode inside.

When I opened it up, I understood why.

There, scrawled in blue pen, was Carla's message: *867-5309.*

———————————-

The boss and I didn't say anything during the train ride back, nor when we finally rolled out sleeping bags in the cargo bay to get some rest, just as the first of Greenly's two suns came over the horizon.

I woke up, smoked a cigarette, and ate one of our ship's complement of banana-flavored energy bars. It took two trips around the cargo bay looking at the damage in the daylight before I realized the boss's sleeping bag lay empty. I checked the cockpit and ship exterior, but he was nowhere to be found. Figuring he must have gotten an early start hunting down repair parts, I set to work looking for the coolant leak.

By the time I heard the boss climb aboard, I was covered in grease and grime and soaked in a foul-smelling combination of sweat and reactor coolant.

"Yo, Bossman, I found where all the coolant went," I called up to him from where I lay amidships—in a shallow pool of blue coolant, wedged uncomfortably in the claustrophobia-inducing crawlspace between the ship's floor and outer hull. "Turns out we didn't vent it all out. The fire in filter bank five ruptured the main line down here and it's all over the place. Primary heat sinks aren't damaged, though, which is good, but I think it shorted out the—"

The boss poked his head into the crawlspace maintenance hatch. "I found her, Snake. I found out where she's at," he called.

"Uh huh," I grunted, more than a bit pissed he'd been out looking for Carla while I toiled away trying to fix things. "Awesome. Great. Real happy for you. So why aren't you there getting all your questions answered?"

"Because I'm gonna need your help. She's over at Joey Machete's, and that isn't the kind of place you walk into alone."

"Yeah, well, I dunno if you noticed, but I'm a little busy right now."

"C'mon, Snake. She's at a meeting and she's not gonna be there all day. This is probably our only chance to get some answers from her."

"Fine. Fuckin' fine," I muttered as I wiggled my way down the crawlspace toward the maintenance hatch, scraping my back on the number two junction box as I did so. "I'll just stop what I'm doing and go help you track down your manic pixie dream girl bounty hunter who obviously doesn't want to be found so you can ask her some questions she obviously doesn't want to answer."

I squeezed through the tiny maintenance hatch and up into the crew cabin, coming face to face with my boss, who was as clean as I was dirty.

I eyed him with suspicion. "What happened to you?"

"What?" he asked.

I folded my arms across my chest and gave him a *really?* look.

He glanced down at his clothes. "Oh, this. Yeah, I did some laundry and took a shower at the service station this morning. You shouldn't've slept in so late. Now come on."

"I am dirty as shit from the coolant and whatever the hell else is down there in the subfloor and you just want me to hop on the train?" I asked. "Hell no. I need a shower something bad and—"

"We don't have time, Snake. Just change into something else and come on, for fuck's sake. Stop being such a baby. You aren't going on a date."

CHAPTER EIGHT

Clean clothes didn't help my smell very much, and by the time we got off the train, my arms and legs had developed a funny sort of tingle as the coolant soaked into my skin. I did my best to ignore it as I followed the boss through a desolate industrial district until we crossed another set of railroad tracks and followed a dead-end street to the gleaming art-deco building at its end. A vintage-style neon sign read *Joey Machete's* in hot pink, glowing brightly even in the light of Greenly's second sun. Several taxis and more than a few expensive late-model performance cars parked in the street out front told me even though it was too early in the day for the club scene, Joey Machete's was doing brisk business.

I looked at the boss. "First, she's *here*? And second, where is *here*?"

"Apparently this is the biggest bounty hunter club in the whole sector."

"Like Anne Marie's over on Diis?" I asked.

He nodded. "Yeah. Pretty much. Took a bit of asking around, but I ran into an engine mechanic who works for the Tanaka Corporation at a diner this morning who recognized my description of Carla. He—"

"Wait. You got up, got clean, *and* had a sit-down breakfast? While I've been crawling around in the subfloor?"

"Listen, you want to hear this or what?" he asked. "Anyway, apparently Carla comes over here for meetings with Tanaka every time he's in town. He said Tanaka got in last night, just after we did, so I found the club's number and asked to speak to Carla."

"And?"

"They offered to take a message."

"You know, boss, that is actually a good bit of detective work," I said, impressed.

"Yeah. Pretty proud of it myself. But here's the deal. While I don't think this is a members only type club, I do think they're not going to take too kindly to me showing up here during 'bounty hunter hours' asking questions, so watch my back, would ya?"

As we did our best to act like we belonged while walking toward the front door, a worrisome thought struck me.

"Hey, boss, did we ever pay back the money we owed Bouelle? You know, for the—"

The boss shrugged. "Eh. Most of it?"

The hulking doorman didn't open the door for us, but he didn't stop us from entering either, which I took as a positive sign. Once inside, we stood in an ornately tiled anteroom, the entrance to the club itself barred by two massive wooden doors and flanked by two equally massive bouncers, one white and one black, who made the tough out front look small by comparison. Above the club doors was a wooden sign with brass letters that read *No unauthorized weapons. Violators will be handled by club security.*

It didn't take a genius to figure out that anybody who got "handled" by the two guarding the door would be lucky to leave with all their limbs attached.

The boss must have been thinking the same, because he faltered for a step as he asked "So, uh, what exactly makes a weapon unauthorized?"

"If you have to ask, yours is," the dark-skinned bouncer told the boss. "Hand it over."

The boss surrendered his pistol and the guard deposited it in a hidden drawer recessed into the wall. The bouncer handed him a claim ticket.

I tried walking through, but a meaty white hand on my chest stopped me.

"You too, pal," the white bouncer told me. I gave up my knife up as well.

We stepped through the anteroom doors and into a vast wood paneled room, dimly lit save for an empty stage illuminated by brilliant white arc lights above. To our left, the bartender looked up at us from a bar that seemed to stretch for kilometers before he went back to his work washing glasses. The whole place reminded me of a movie set.

"I dunno about you," I whispered to the boss as we took seats at the otherwise empty bar, "but I don't think this is my kind of place."

"Yeah, you ain't kidding," he agreed. "But we aren't here for a good time. As soon as I make sure our six is clear, it's back to the ship and back to work."

"Speaking of work, boss, what do you think the exposure limit on coolant is? My arms are starting to tingle and my whole lower body is numb."

"You'll be fine," he replied. "I'm sure it's not good for you, but as much as you smoke and drink and as bad as you shoot, something else is bound to kill you first."

"Easy for you to say," I muttered as I moved my numb right foot just to make sure I still could.

I was into my third bourbon by the time I spotted Carla as she descended the darkened staircase beside the bar. She chatted with a silver-haired black man whose attire and swagger screamed "high-end bounty hunter." For some reason, I'd expected she'd be wearing the same form-fitting flight suit as before, but instead she wore a pair of tight blue jeans and stylish red blouse with a keyhole cutout that couldn't help but catch my eye. I also noticed that unlike us, she hadn't had to check her pistol at the door.

"Yo, boss, there she is," I said with a nod in her direction.

"I see her," he said as he polished off his scotch. "Let's go have a chat."

He hopped off his stool and I did the same, although whether because the stuff I was drinking was better than I was used to or because of the lingering effects of coolant-poisoning, I felt like I moved in slow motion. I shook my head to clear it and caught up with the boss at the foot of the staircase.

Carla stopped mid-sentence when she saw us, surprise obvious on her face.

"What are you two doing here?"

"We've still got questions that need answering," the boss said.

"I told you where to find me," Carla said flatly. "And it wasn't here."

"Yeah—*867-5309*? That was real funny. Real fucking funny," the boss said. "But it doesn't matter, 'cause we're right here, right now."

The first genuine smile I'd seen yet flashed across Carla's face, but it disappeared as quickly as it had come.

"These two a problem, Carla?" the bounty hunter asked in a tone of voice that suggested if she gave the word, we wouldn't be a problem much longer.

"Don't worry about it, Rick. I can handle 'em. Believe it or not, they really are here just to ask questions."

"Fair enough," Rick said as he stepped between the boss and I to take a seat at the bar.

"Well? Find a table so we can get this over with," Carla said.

Carla and I followed the boss to a booth. I sat down first, glad to be off my tingling, unsteady legs. Carla slid into the booth across from me. For a second, it looked as if the boss was going to try to sit beside her, but an icy look from Carla sent him scurrying around to my side of the table.

I snorted and the boss shot me a dirty look.

"All right," Carla sighed. "So, what's up?"

"Tell us what the job was—the real job," the boss demanded.

"Wow. Right down to business huh?" she asked with a smirk. "Not much for foreplay, I see."

"From him? Oh, God, no," I said. "That's *my* department." If a look could kill, the boss's glare would have dropped me dead on the spot.

"Just answer the damn question, Carla," he said.

"Fine. There was a bounty on Patrick Anders, the so-called 'Tyrant of Tellerson.' His crew isn't the only bunch in the system, but they are the biggest and the toughest. For a few years now, Mr. Tanaka has had a deal with Anders, where he paid to have his ships get through without getting ripped."

"I'm guessing something went sideways," the boss observed.

"Yeah. About six months ago, Anders expanded his operation into Bascia. He knocked off two Tanaka Corporation shipments from Paulus to Kagawa-ken in the first week. Mr. Tanaka saw that as a breach of the agreement and sent word to Anders demanding he cover the cost of the shipments. Anders said the existing agreement only covered ships in Tellison and if Tanaka didn't want his ships getting hit in Bascia, the price was going to go up."

"Ah. And Mr. Tanaka had a problem with that," I said.

"You could say that," Carla said.

"Did you forget you only talk to captains?" I asked with a grin.

She laughed—a real, charming laugh, the kind we'd heard over the radio aboard the *Recovery Star*. "Shit. Actually, yeah, I did. You got me. But that's the last time. Besides, the mission's over anyway." Carla waved a hand at me with a smile.

I felt the heat of the boss's glare, but didn't acknowledge it as I pressed on. "I get it: Mr. Tanaka doesn't want to pay Anders, so he puts a bounty on his head. But what the hell does that have to do with you hiring us to go out there and get killed?"

"It's more complicated than that," Carla said. "Because after Anders refused to honor the deal, that's where me, Maria, and Rick come in. Mr. Tanaka hired us to clean Anders out of Bascia, which we did. I got one of his crew at nav point twelve and Maria took out a pair of 'em coming out of the T53. Rick worked planetside down here and took out Anders's group that were watching the spaceport and passing him info on ships' flight plans and destinations. After that, Anders sent word that he would honor the agreement again and we thought everything was cool."

"Still doesn't explain why you hired us," the boss pointed out.

"I'm getting there. After things looked quiet, Mr. Tanaka disbanded us and we went on our way. Thing is, Anders wasn't really done. He sent his son Roscoe after Maria. He got her in Pinewood, just like they said out there on the radio. Mr. Tanaka was furious."

"Part of the job, though," the boss said. "What does a big businessman care if one of his hired guns gets killed?"

"The Bascia contract was my first job with Mr. Tanaka, but Rick and Maria had done work off and on for Mr. Tanaka for years. He considered them part of the family and felt like Anders knew, and that's why he'd gone after Maria—so Mr. Tanaka decided to pay Anders back in kind."

"He killed Roscoe," I said.

"Yep. Rick smoked him—and two of his bodyguards—on Del Rio Station. Mr. Tanaka knew that would be war, so he brought me back on, told me to round up a cargo boat as bait, and sent me to make the Tellison-Markins run and bring him back proof Anders was dead."

"Jesus, so we really were just bait," the boss huffed. "Why not just fly to Tellison and get him yourself instead of dragging us into it? You didn't need us out there."

"If I would have flown out there alone I never would'a found 'em. They weren't gonna come out and jump a single Razor. That would mark me as an obvious bounty hunter, and they get nothing out of tangling with a hunter just for kicks. I needed you two to sell the idea it was a legit shipment. Besides, while I probably didn't *need* you out there, you were more helpful than I thought, actually. Snake there isn't a half-bad gunner."

I reclined back in the booth and folded my hands behind my head. "Yep. I'm good with my hands," I said with a wink. I couldn't help it. Even though Carla had nearly gotten us killed, I couldn't resist the opening.

She chuckled. "Oh really?"

"Oh, yeah. I hear it all the time. I'll schedule you a personal demo sometime."

She rolled her eyes but smiled anyway.

Despite everything bad I'd previously said about her and that she'd come *this close* to getting us killed, I had a newfound liking for the pretty bounty hunter.

Judging by the look on the boss's face, he did not approve of my recently developed verdict on Carla.

"He's not good. He's lucky, that's all," the boss said with a scowl.

Carla shrugged. "Anyway, where was I? Oh, yeah. Once they came out of the nebula for you, I just pretended to be Maria—which was easy 'cause even though she was supposed to be dead, they'd never met her in person, and all they knew was she flew a Razor, too—and sent them Rick's picture of Roscoe's corpse, hoping to get a response from Anders so I could confirm he was on their mothership I was about to waste. I got the confirmation I needed, kicked his ass, and that was that. Contract fulfilled."

"About that," the boss said, eyes narrowed. "Just how much did you make on this contract?"

Carla gave the boss a mischievous smile and shook her head. "You should'a thought of all these questions back there in the bar instead of trying to imagine what I look like without my flight suit on."

The boss went red, but to his credit, he kept on with his line of questioning. "Never mind that. How much did you make?"

She turned and yelled to the bounty hunter at the bar. "Hey, Rick, what's the standard finder's fee?"

"Ten percent," he called back.

Carla turned back to us.

"*Ten percent?*" the boss hissed. "You got paid a hundred-and-fifty grand and we get a lousy fifteen k? What the hell kind of deal is that?"

"Industry standard, ace. You want something different, you gotta negotiate ahead of time. Consider that free life advice."

"I probably took forty thou worth of damage helping you find your man," the boss fumed.

"Boo-fucking-hoo," Carla said. "You want charity, go stand on a street corner. You need a loan? Swing by and we'll talk terms. But bottom line is, I offered you the job and you took it. Now, I'm going to get a drink."

She slid out of the booth. As I watched her go, I found myself doing what she'd accused the boss of doing—wondering what she looked like without her flight suit on.

"Oh, no you don't," the boss said with an elbow in my ribs. "I've seen that look before. Forget it. What was it you said? 'You think she's sex on legs but she's nothing but trouble in a flight suit' or something? You were absolutely one-hundred-ten-fucking-percent right, okay? So now that I've said it, forget about Carla and let's get back to the ship and get to work."

I had to admit, he was probably right, if only because he was quoting me and I'm almost *always* right.

He exited the booth and I did the same, wincing when I put weight on my legs. They felt like they'd fallen asleep, except the pins-and-needles feeling wasn't going away.

"Shit, boss, I wasn't kidding about that coolant exposure, man. I can't feel my legs."

"Oh, come on, Snake. You can take a shower when you get back."

"No, seriously," I said. "You close the tab at the bar and I'm going to the bathroom. I gotta try to wash some of this shit off before I get any worse than I am already."

"Fine," he said. "But don't take forever, all right? We got a lot to do."

Inside the immaculate bathroom, I stripped off my boots and pants. My skin was red and splotchy and cool to the touch. Slapping my leg didn't hurt at all, but it also didn't remove the tingling numbness. I used paper towels and warm water to try to clean my skin, and with each pass, the towels came away the faint blue color of Quaralene, our engine coolant of choice.

I frowned in the mirror, knowing that in a few hours I'd likely be puking and shitting my brains out as my body tried to purge itself of the toxins. I'd been through this before, years ago when I was on the *Braxton,* so while I was pretty sure it wouldn't kill me, I knew it sure was gonna feel like it. I wet another paper towel and wiped my legs again.

Shouts from the club caught my attention and I froze. I couldn't tell what was going on exactly, but it didn't sound good. I put my pants back on and crept back out into the club in my bare feet. As I did, I reached reflexively for my knife before I realized it was still in the drawer where I'd left it with security.

Shit.

My eyes hadn't fully readjusted from the bathroom light to the club's darkness, but far across the club floor, I could make out Rick sitting at the bar perfectly still, and the boss standing with his hands at chest level, raised and open. Carla sat at the same table we'd just left, hands atop the table. One figure I didn't recognize stood in the gloom pointing what I guessed was a pistol at Rick and the boss while another towered over Carla at the table. Neither one of them seemed to have noticed me, so I made my way closer from table to table, crouched low to stay in the dim murk of Joey Machete's.

"That's right, Rick," the one closest to the bar said. "You keep both hands where I can see 'em, and you just might live through this. Our beef ain't with you."

"Do you know where you are?" Rick asked before he took a long slow sip of beer. "Because you have just made a *very* big mistake."

"We didn't ask you for your opinion, because we don't care," the one at the table said. "What we care about is who it was that got Anders and the rest. First, we heard it was Maria, but that can't be right, 'cause she's dead. Then I heard a rumor going around it was some other bitch in a Razor, flyin' with a merchie on her wing. And this got me thinking: where did the cute chick who worked for Tanaka go? And here she is. What a surprise."

"If you leave now, Mr. Tanaka may let this slide," Rick warned. "But the longer you stick around, the less chance there is of that."

"Shut your fuckin' mouth, Rick," the one at the bar said. "Else I'll shut it permanently."

"And who are you, flyboy?" the man at the table called out, gesturing with a silver pistol to my boss. "You ain't a regular, seeing your pistol's checked. Maybe you own that shot-up Black Sun the tug boys told me they towed in from Tellison? Now wouldn't that be something?"

"What do you want?" Carla asked. "Anders is dead. You shooting us won't change that, and I know nobody liked the shithead enough to put a bounty on me for killing him."

The man at Carla's table laughed. "Yeah, we know, but now that Anders is dead, we're out of a paycheck, so we figured you could help. What we want is the money you got for killing him, and maybe a little something else besides. So, hand over the cashcard and come without a fuss and things'll go fine, or else I'll find it when I take it off your corpse."

While he talked, I sized him up. He was tall and lanky, with a pistol in his right hand and an assault knife—the kind with a stiletto blade and a stun gun in the handle—in his left. I'd have felt better about the whole situation if I had my own trusty E-14 knife, but this business rarely gives you good odds.

I stole another table nearer, close enough to the table for Carla to notice me. Her eyes widened. She gave me a barely perceptible nod.

"So? You coming, or should I just shoot you now?" the man at the table asked.

"Fine," Carla said. "I'll go with you, but leave Rick and the merchie out of it."

"Fuck that," said the one at the bar. "Flyboy here got paid, same as you did. We're taking his share too. Hand over your cashcard."

"Whoa, now," the boss said. "I don't even have all of it—"

"What the fuck did you say?" the assailant closest to Carla's table screamed. "The *fuck* did you say? You don't have it? Well too fuckin' bad, dumbass, 'cause we're gonna get it one way or another. Lucas, fuck him right up, and make sure he remembers—"

I leapt out of the dark, grabbing the man's gun hand with my left hand and his knife hand with my right. At the same time, I kneed him in the groin and drove him to the floor.

His pistol fired once as we fell, then skittered off into the darkness when we landed.

His left hand slipped free and I rolled off him to avoid getting stabbed, giving him an elbow to the face as I did so.

He rolled with me, and in the dark I saw he no longer had the knife. I dodged a punch and grabbed his face, pressing my right thumb into his left eye as far as I could.

He screamed and jerked back.

I heard an incoherent shout from the bar followed by a pair of gunshots. The man I'd attacked struggled off me and tried to stand, but I grabbed his belt and yanked him down again. As he fell, he threw a wild haymaker that caught me in the jaw. I saw stars and let go of his belt.

There was a deafening gun blast from Carla's position at the table, then more commotion at the bar.

The man I fought stumbled to his feet, gave me a swift kick to the ribs, and turned to run.

Pop. The entire room flashed red. *Pop.* The room went red again, and everything was quiet.

I looked toward the bar to see Rick standing next to his stool, beer in his left hand and laz pistol in his right, barrel glowing cherry red. The charred corpse of the attacker at the bar lay sprawled out between him and Carla's table, and the incinerated body of the man I'd tussled with was a cinder-black shadow on the floor.

"You all right over there?" he called.

My legs felt even more numb than they had before and my heart pounded a thousand beats a minute from the adrenaline, but I found my way to my feet. I stepped into the light of the bar, a triumphant smile on my face.

"I'm alive, how about you guys?"

Rick nodded, but the boss looked like he was going to be sick.

"Well, I'll give you credit," Carla said from her table. "You're a lot sneakier than I figured. And a tough motherfucker too." She pointed at my right leg.

I looked down to see the combat knife buried hilt-deep in my thigh, pulsing with each heartbeat. Blood soaked my pants and little rivers of it ran down my leg and over my bare foot.

"Shit."

I passed out.

CHAPTER NINE

I woke up on the train, sitting in a wheelchair.

"Welcome back," the boss said.

"Shit. What happened?"

"You passed out."

"Yeah, no shit," I said. "I meant after that."

The boss leaned back in his seat. "Well, Mr. Tanaka came downstairs with his bodyguards and several other heavies came out from side rooms and whatnot and pronounced an all-out motherfuckin' war on anybody who'd ever even *thought* about helping Anders, going all the way back to his grade school teachers I think."

"Where the fuck was club security the whole time?" I asked, cautiously running my hand down my leg, checking to see if the wound still hurt.

"Outside man was dead. The other two'd been zapped and cuffed. Tanaka worked 'em over pretty good, but they'll live."

"Jesus. I'll take my chances at the shitty little bars we hang out in any day of the week," I said.

"Yeah."

"Where'd Carla go?"

The boss shot me an annoyed look. "She split. Haven't seen her in the two days since. Haven't been looking for her either."

"*Two days?* I've been out for two whole days?"

"In and out, but, yeah, pretty much."

"Shit."

"Yep. Only good thing that came out of all this was that one of those two assholes had a bounty."

I smiled. "Oh really? How much?"

"Seven grand."

"Sweet. That'll help us out—"

"Split three ways," the boss interrupted.

"Oh."

"Yeah, and your hospital bill was over three and a half."

"Damn it! Just to patch up my leg? They charged that much?"

The boss avoided my eyes. "Well, that and some other stuff."

"Other stuff? Like what?"

"Apparently the amount of Quaralene you'd absorbed through your skin was at, um, 'near fatal levels' I think is how they put it. The detox is what cost most of the cash."

"I *told* you, asshole. I told you I needed a shower. I told you I didn't feel good, I *told* you. But no, you were all 'you'll be fine, Snake, quit whining.' I swear, when we get back to the ship, it's gonna be your ass crawling through the toxic soup down in the subfloor."

"Yeah, yeah, yeah," he said. "I've already been down in it actually. I fixed the leak, got the system recharged and got the number three engine running. Number two isn't far from being back up either."

"Well, that's good news. What about number one?"

He shook his head. "Needs a total rebuild. And I haven't even started on all the sensors and fire damage. Or the radiation shields. Or the ECM module, or the targeting system, or comms, or—"

"We got a lot of work to do. I get it, man, but—"

"I don't think you do," the boss said as he slumped against the train window. "I'm out of cash. Almost flat broke."

"Shit, man. If I had any cash to give you, I would, but—"

"What about that line you gave me back on Ramseur, about loaning me the money to fix the targeting system?" he asked.

"Are you stupid? Don't you think I would've already forked it over if I had it? You think I would *choose* to fly on a ship without a targeting system? C'mon, boss. I got like three hundred credits to my name, for real."

"I dunno, I was hoping you had a rich uncle or something."

I snorted. "Rich uncles are *your* department."

A rich uncle. Right. The boss was the one with the connections. Although he'd always been evasive about it, I had pieced together the fact he'd grown up rich and his father was some kind of powerful political bigshot. I rubbed my face and considered the possibility.

"Here's how I see it," the boss said. "We've still got enough to use the elevator, so we—"

"We could borrow it from your dad, couldn't we?" I suggested.

"No. He wouldn't loan it and I wouldn't ask. Forget it."

"I just figured—"

"I literally would *rather die* than ask for money from my father. He's him, and I'm me," the boss replied, serious as a lock warning.

"But we—"

"End of discussion, Snake."

I let it drop.

"Fine. So, what's the plan?"

"Like I was saying, we use the elevator to get back out of orbit, since we can't with just two engines. I've got enough to cover the fee one way. Then, we'll take an insys run to the T53 Outpost— has to be there because the heat shields are too busted for reentry—and use the cash we got to repair the radiation shields, which have to be the first—"

"You wanna do a deep space run when our radiation shields are shredded? Are you out of your mind? We'll be glowing before we reach the second nav point."

"The radiation won't be that high, as long as there's no solar flares," the boss said with a dismissive shrug. "We'll be all right for one run."

"And what, just pray we don't get jumped? Because we'll have no targeting, no ECM, no port shields, and be limping along with two engines. Jesus fuck, man, listen to yourself! You're talking about a suicide mission to make probably fifteen-hundred credits—*tops*. And even if we *could* afford to buy radiation shields on T53 after the run, could we even afford the docking charges?"

"We'd have to skip out on 'em," the boss said. "But we've done that before in other places."

"Yeah, but when we did that before we weren't limping along held together by vacuum tape and a prayer, boss. Plus, it's kind of a bad idea to cut yourself off from *the only place you can land*, remember? We still won't have our heat shields for reentry."

"I know. That's why, after we make the first run to T53, we head for Diis. Big station, plenty of work, even in-system."

In my time flying for him, my boss had had a lot of dangerous ideas, and a lot of big, stupid plans, but this had to be the biggest, stupidest, most dangerous plan ever. I remembered telling him that about his decision to do the Tellison-Markins run, but the way I saw it, we'd have better odds doing that *twice* than reaching Diis in our current state.

"Diis is what, six or seven jumps away?" I did the calculations in my head. "Twelve days, I think—no wait, we're on two engines, so more like fifteen or twenty. Through Xiamen and Hadris. Without targeting or portside shields. Or ECM. With CO_2 scrubbing at fifty percent. Hell, even if by some miracle we did make it through, when we landed on Diis we wouldn't even have the cash to cover the landing fees, which means they'd impound the ship as soon as we showed up. No thanks, I think I'm better off flapping my arms and hoping to turn into a bird."

"Goddamn it, at least I'm trying to think of something instead of just shooting everything down. What's your solution then, Snake?" the boss asked.

"I dunno, man, but not any of that."

"You're a ton of help," he replied, his voice cutting. "Tell you what, when we get back to the ship, you work and I'll think."

"Pretty sure it was your thinking that got us into this mess, boss," I shot back, and regretted it as soon the words left my mouth.

He didn't reply, but his jaw clenched tight and he stared out the window. He didn't say anything the rest of the trip.

When we got to our stop, I had to wheel myself out of the train.

———————————————————·

Three days of solid work under our belts had improved things somewhat, but there was still tension in the air. I could get around without the wheelchair, but my leg still hurt and I moved "like old people fuck," as the boss put it. My lack of mobility left me doing the work behind the ship's computers or trying to do research on how to fix problems, which was usually the boss's job, and left him crawling around, replacing things, running tests, and getting dirty. I never would have admitted it to him, but he was a damn sight better at doing my job than I was at doing his.

Unfortunately, given our lack of funds, we'd all but exhausted what we could actually fix, so we wound up spending a lot of time fixing minor problems because the major problems were too big to contemplate. That's how I found myself smoking cigarettes in the cockpit, checking voltage levels, and reading out of a maintenance procedure book to the boss while he crammed himself half inside the midship computer cabinet.

"*Step four,*" I read, "*Place circuit breaker twelve in off position.*"

"Done," the boss called, voice muffled by the metal cabinet.

"*Set mode switch to alternate.*"

"Yep."

"Okay, now at my station, I set the mode to test," I told him. I selected *test* from the menu I'd called up on the VDU. "Then it says… ah—okay, *blinking yellow light indicates no fault. Solid yellow light indicates fault and*—"

"I got a solid yellow light," the boss said. "Of course."

"Yep. So now, you press the test button on the panel and read me the voltage and—"

"I show point two-seven-five," he interrupted.

"And I check the voltage up here, which is… One-point-one."

"Shit," he said. "That's out of tolerance, isn't it?"

"Yeah. Manual says tolerance level is point one-five. And if it's greater, the relay has to be replaced."

I heard him mutter something under his breath and flip a switch. "Okay, what are you showing now?" he asked.

I took another drag from my cigarette before I answered. "Still showing one-point-one, Boss."

"Fuck. Let me try something else. Hold on. How about now?"

The numbers on my screen didn't change. "Nope. Still the same."

He flipped a circuit breaker on and off. "That might clear it. Any different?"

I blew a cloud of smoke at the computer screen. "No. Still one-point-one. It's hopeless, Boss. The relay has to be replaced."

"God-fucking-*damn*-it. Can't I get just one, teeny, tiny, fucking break? Is that too much to ask for?" he yelled from inside the cabinet.

He emerged from the cabinet, banging his head on the door as he did so. I turned around in the cockpit to ask him a question and was surprised to see him stomping out the rear hatch and into the cargo bay, headed for the open bay door.

"What are you doing?" I called.

"What difference does it make?" he shouted. "Like you said, Snake, 'it's hopeless.'"

He stomped off toward the tram station. I settled into the cockpit and lit another cigarette.

I didn't see him again for four days.

When he came back, he looked wrung out. He had broken blood vessels around his eyes and the hollow look of a man who'd had too much to drink and too little to eat for several days running. He held a handle of cheap vodka in each hand.

"*Jesus*, Boss. What the hell happened to you?"

He didn't answer and made his way past where I sat in the cargo bay next to a pile of cigarette butts, sorting a huge bunch of mixed fuses by amperage. He collapsed onto the couch amidships and stretched out.

"I heard there's a brothel just out of the city. You find a girl you liked?" I joked.

"Not in the mood, Snake."

I nodded. "Okay, fair. But seriously, where have you been?"

"I went and saw a guy I heard about."

I waited for him to say more, but he seemed content to leave it there. I wasn't. I lit another cigarette and walked into the crew cabin where I extended the pack to him.

"Cigarette?"

"Nah." He unscrewed the cap off one of the bottles of vodka. "That shit's bad for you."

"Uh *huh*," I said as I watched him take a long swig. "So come on, man, out with it. What's up?"

"Guy I went to see was Eric Keena. You know the name?"

"Never heard of him."

"He's the local guy for the Sevens."

My blood went cold. The Triple Sevens were the oldest criminal organization in the Outer Systems, with a well-earned reputation for efficiency and brutality. They were the kinds of gangsters even other gangsters steered clear of.

"Tell me you did not make a deal with the Sevens," I pleaded. "Those aren't the kind of deals you walk away from. Dealing with the Sevens is how you wind up with people like Rick tracking you down. Tell me we're not mixed up with—"

"No. No, they offered me a loan, but even as stupid drunk as I was, I knew the juice was too much. I just knew two months from now I'd miss a payment, and a week after they'd be chopping off my fingers in some basement in Neo-Beijing. No, I didn't take the deal."

I breathed a sigh of relief. "Thanks for that, 'cause I like having all my digits."

"It's kind of funny," he mused after he took another long pull. "It took me a day to get drunk enough to work up the courage to say yes and then two days to get drunk enough to face the fact I'd said no."

"So where does that leave us, ship-wise?"

"Fuck if I know, Snake. All I know is I'm gonna drink these two bottles of vodka and see if they make things any better. Feel free to help."

"And if that doesn't work?" I asked, taking a pull from the bottle.

"Go buy two more bottles, I guess."

CHAPTER TEN

The vodka did not make things better.

I awoke the following afternoon, sprawled out beside my sleeping bag in the cargo bay, vomit all around me. The smell almost made me throw up again. The boss occupied the ship's latrine, alternating between puking and cursing.

My head felt like somebody had slammed it in a car door and my breath tasted like a pack of wild dogs had shit in my mouth. I pressed the door release on the cargo bay and wobbled outside, where I promptly threw up when the bright light of Greenly's second sun hit my eyes.

"You know what, Snake?" the boss called from the latrine.

"What?" I asked.

"I don't think the vodka did any good. And even though I said I'd buy two more bottles, I don't think I wanna do this again. Not for a few days, at least."

"Yeah. Right there with you, Boss."

Since we'd managed to get the ship's life support circulation back running, the ship had clean water, courtesy of the utility hookups at the pad. Furthermore, since I'd replaced most of the blown fuses in the boss's absence, the ship had *hot* water, which meant I could take a shower in the tiny shower closet.

Once I did, and after I'd changed into my last set of clean clothes, I felt much better. I smoked a cigarette and watched the second sunset from the open cargo bay door. The boss sat where I had several days earlier, sorting the dwindling pile of fuses.

"I'm going out," I announced.

"Where to?" he asked.

"I dunno. I just need a walk, now that I can again. And I need to get out of the ship for a bit.

There's a couple of restaurants off the first tram stop from here. I'll grab us some wings or something. Gotta get something in my stomach and I can't eat another damn banana energy bar right now."

"Snake, man, listen," the boss said, his tone serious. "If you gotta…" He trailed off.

"What?"

"If you gotta go, man, and take a job on another ship, I understand, man. I really do. No hard feelings or anything. You got no money and you're flying with a guy who's got no money and no ship, so really, I get it if you gotta go. I'll even give you a good reference."

"I'll be back, Bossman, don't sweat it," I said as I finished my cigarette. "And if I wasn't, I sure as fuck wouldn't list you as a reference. I know *I* wouldn't hire anybody who'd worked for you."

"Get the fuck outta here, Snake," the boss said with a grin.

I took the tram to the first stop, but I didn't feel like going to the restaurant just yet. Instead, I walked out of the concourse and across the street, to the lit sidewalk that ran in front of one of the identical towering apartment complexes that housed most of Greenly's residents.

I looked up at the building, wondering what it would be like to live in one of them. I wondered what it would be like to come home to the same place every day, to always know what was coming, to be able to plan around a consistent schedule, to know the neighbors—hell, to *have* neighbors. I thought about waking up every day and standing out on one of those balconies watching the sunsets while drinking a glass of wine, of a day where my biggest worry was making sure I didn't miss the train.

It all sounded pretty fucking terrible, honestly.

I chuckled as people gave me a wide berth on the sidewalk. Even though I was washed and clean, and even though I was soft as fuck by the standards of my own past, I was still too much for these ground-loving apartment dwellers to take.

I took cover from the wind behind one of the massive lamp posts to light my cigarette, idly reading the notices taped to the post as I did. One of them caught my eye.

MOVING SALE! FRIDAY THROUGH SUNDAY! My husband and I are moving from Greenly City to Jefferson, so we're selling some furniture. Come by anytime this weekend, apt 233-4110.

233-4110.

Something about the number format stood out to me for some reason, but I couldn't—

It hit me.

867-5309.

Holy fuck.

I jogged down the block to the next entrance in the fence surrounding the apartment grounds. Illuminated by the streetlight, a wrought iron sign announced the apartment complex number: *Building 233.*

I remembered something Carla had said at Joey Machete's: *"I told you where to find me."*

I remembered something else, too.

Carla had offered us a loan.

————————————

I ran back to the tram station, thoughts of chicken wings abandoned. I hopped aboard and asked another passenger which stop would put me closest to the 867 block of apartments. I followed her instructions and got off ten stops later, near the south spaceport exit where the boss and I had gone to look for Carla's Razor.

From there I walked three blocks east until I stood outside a sleek glass and steel tower, well lit, and displaying *867* in mammoth block letters over its massive bank of revolving doors. I spied an older man struggling with bags of groceries as he exited a taxi, so I grabbed several and carried them toward the door for him, chatting him up along the way. The doorman didn't give me a second look.

Once inside, he showed me where the express elevators were and I took one to the fifty-third floor. From there, I padded down the brightly-lit hallway until I found a door covered in psychedelic purple flowers and a peace sign. It didn't look like how I'd pictured Carla's apartment would look at all, but below a hand-stenciled bullshit flower-power quote about love and understanding or something were four brass numbers: *5309*.

I knocked on the door. I saw the peephole go dark and then the door swung open. I was greeted by a pretty, buxom brunette about Carla's age but a few inches taller. She wore an eye-catching sheer green shirt over a lacy bra and a floor-length skirt made of that trendy fabric that displays holographic fractal patterns.

I was expecting a pretty girl, just not *this* pretty girl, which threw me for a loop. "Ah, hi," I said. "I'm looking for—"

"I know. You're here for Carla. I'm Jade," she said, extending a hand, which I shook. "Come on in."

Inside, the artistic psychedelic theme continued, where Jade set me down on a couch patterned in a multi-colored fabric that made me think of an exploding sun. Jade disappeared into the kitchen. I looked around at the various wall hangings, pictures of elephants in meditative poses, and fancy antique pictures and decided the apartment had to be Jade's, not Carla's.

Jade called to me from the kitchen.

"Need a drink?"

My stomach rumbled at the mere suggestion of alcohol.

"I appreciate the offer, but no thanks. Last night was a rough one."

She laughed. "I know the feeling."

"Jade," Carla called from a room somewhere behind me. "Is my green dress still in the laundry?"

"I don't know," Jade answered as she came back from the kitchen holding a gin and tonic. "It wasn't my week to do it, remember? By the way, your date's here."

My head snapped around to tell Jade she had the situation *way* wrong, but she'd already disappeared down the hallway.

"What?" Carla said, frustration in her voice. "He's like thirty minutes early. Why the fuck is he here already?"

"I dunno," Jade called as she walked back around the corner. "But he's cute enough." She winked at me.

I sat up a little straighter.

"He damn well better be, showing up half an hour early."

I heard a door open and Carla walked around the corner. In the time since I'd last seen her, she'd re-dyed her hair, which was now a light blue that brought out her green eyes. She wore matching lipstick and earrings and carried a bottle of nail polish the same color. She had on skin-tight blue jeans and an emerald shirt with a plunging V-neck that came almost to her navel. I struggled to keep my eyes from drifting down her chest.

Her face registered complete surprise for a second, before she broke out into a smirk.

"What are *you* doing here?"

Jade came back around the corner, fury on her face. "I thought that was your date?"

Carla gave Jade a sidelong glance. "*This* guy? Ha. No. This guy's nickname is *Snake*. He is *not* dating material. No. He is a business associate. Technically, an associate of a one-time associate. Besides, I thought you said he was cute." She delivered the last line with a sly smile that raised the temperature of the room several degrees.

"Get out, you son of a bitch!" Jade snapped at me, her earlier easy hospitality nowhere to be found. "Get out of my apartment."

I held up my hands but didn't move off the couch. "Whoa there, Jade, calm down. I never said I was Carla's date. *You* said that. As Carla said, I'm a business associate. And I was invited, kind of. The only reason I even know where to find her is because she gave me her apartment number."

"I *told* you not to bring what you do here, Carla," Jade said. "That negative energy disrupts the sacred peace of this space."

Carla glanced at me and rolled her eyes. "You did tell me that. And I'm sorry, okay? But I had to be somewhere, and Snake and his boss had questions for me but something else came up, so I left the apartment number. Of course, they were too clueless to figure out that's what it was, so they never showed up that night."

"I don't care, Carla—he's got to go."

Carla shook her head. "All right, all right, a deal's a deal. I know. Just let me put some shoes on and I'll take a walk and find out what he wants. Away from the 'sacred peace of the space' or whatever."

She disappeared back down the hallway and emerged a minute later. "Come on," she said,

motioning me to follow her. I needed no
encouragement.

"If my date shows up and I'm not back, tell him
I'm handling a business matter and I'll be back in a
few minutes, okay?"

"Sure, Carla," Jade said, flatly. I could tell she
still wasn't over me coming to the apartment.

"Hey, Jade," Carla said with a frown. "I don't
have time to look for that dress, so I'm just gonna
wear what I've got on. Looks good enough, don't
you think?"

"Sure, Carla."

I made a show of looking Carla over. "If I was
your date, *I* wouldn't complain." My eyes met hers
and I gave her the winningest smile I had.

"Wipe that shit-eating grin off your face and
let's get this talk over with," she said, but there was
a note of satisfaction in her voice.

She chuckled, turned, and walked out the door.
I followed and Jade slammed it shut behind us.

"Jesus," I said with a look at the door. "For
being all about love and oneness, she sure is
uptight."

"Jade's like that about bounty hunting," Carla
said as she started off down the hall. "We go back a
few years, and she's known what I do from the
beginning, but she's never liked it. She's just trying

to look out for me. I got a lotta bad history in my line of work."

"I know how that goes," I said as I followed her.

"Oh yeah?"

"Yeah. I wasn't always a loser gunner roaming The Fringe, barely eking out a living."

She turned to face me and rolled her eyes, no doubt ready for me to spin her some bullshit story of greatness. She'd played this game before.

But so had I.

"Nope, you shoulda seen me before," I said, delivering the line in a haughty voice. "Because back then, I was a loser *staying put* in The Fringe, barely eking out a living," I finished with a grin.

"Glad to see you've stayed true to your roots, then," Carla said dryly as she led me through double doors outside onto a communal balcony.

"Yeah, that's why I'm here, in fact," I said, serious again.

She leaned against the chest-high railing and looked down. I took a place beside her and did the same.

"How so?"

"I actually came here looking for a—"

Carla's right eyebrow went up, skepticism written across her face. "Looking for a what?

"For a—"

I hope you're not about to say a date, because you'd be a loser there too," she interrupted with a mischievous smile.

"Har. Not the way I see it."

"*What?*" Carla asked. "Please. I think we both know I'm good at getting what I want—just like I got what I wanted from your boss. And then, out of everybody in this city—no offense—you think *you're* the one who's just gonna show up and I'm gonna go out with you?"

"And yet, here you are," I said, gesturing to the streetlights and spaceport below. "Standing out on the balcony with me."

"Are your eyes brown?" she asked. "Because you're full of shit, you know that, Snake?"

"Yes, and yes."

We both laughed.

"But seriously," she said. "Why are you here? And what took you so long?"

"Well, as you obviously know, your—or Jade's, I guess—apartment number shares a number with a pretty damn famous song, so when the guard handed us that piece of paper, we were pretty sure you were just fucking with us, so we never bothered trying to figure out if you were serious. So that's what took so long."

"I *was* fucking with you guys. I figured I'd already been more than helpful enough, and your boss seemed like the type for long goodbyes. I could'a made it clearer, but I really didn't mind if I never saw you two again."

"Yeah," I said, frowning as I remembered our feelings of rage and frustration that night. "We kinda picked up on that."

She chuckled. "Sorry, but considering you guys showed up at Joey Machete's to ask me a million questions, can you blame me?"

"For the record," I said, "*I* wasn't the one who had the hard on—pardon the pun—for tracking you down. I was perfectly fine with never seeing your ass ever again." I shot a sidelong glance at her and took the risk. "Well, metaphorically speaking, anyway."

She pretended to frown, but her eyes gleamed.

"How long you two been flying together anyway?" she asked, changing the subject to less exciting matters. "You two are a perfect team."

I searched her face for signs she was kidding, but she appeared completely serious.

"I gotta say, I've never heard that one before," I told her.

"Yeah, I figure maybe you two's overlapping stupidity must cancel out or something," she said with a straight face that cracked into a grin.

"You know, just when I was starting to like you."

"Whatever. But seriously, how long have you two flown together?"

I ran through the dates in my head. "Been about five years now, I guess. My previous gig had ended and I was looking for work and a way off Dunatis. He picked me up for a single run and I've been gunning for him ever since."

"It's a wonder you two are still alive."

"You kid, but it's a valid point. I wonder at it myself sometimes. He probably does too. But I'm lucky to have a job at all, all things considered."

"What's that mean?"

"Well, the first time we met I pulled a knife on him and he put a gun under my chin."

"Bullshit," Carla said, incredulous look in her eyes.

"Nope. Serious as a missile lock. Swear to God."

"And he hired you?"

"Yeah. That was kind of the interview, actually." I shrugged. "It's worked out."

"Except for this last run, it seems."

I grimaced. "Yeah."

I knew I should have asked for the loan then and there, but I didn't feel like bringing it up. I was enjoying the pleasant conversation about something other than how bad the boss and I were screwed, something that had been in short supply since we'd landed on Greenly.

"Look," she said. "I'm kind of sorry about how it turned out. Not like sorry enough that I wouldn't do it again, but sorry like I wouldn't laugh quite as hard, you know?"

"I do, actually. I really do." I had never heard someone put my life's philosophy so perfectly.

"Anyway, we can't change what's done," she said with a sigh.

"Yeah. Like you said, bad history. What about you? What's your story, Carla?"

"You know, the usual."

"What's that mean?" I asked.

"The usual. Money trouble, relationship trouble. And despite knowing better, I always seem to fall in with the wrong crowd," she said with a sly smile.

Gunner that I am, I knew it was time to take the shot. "Well, I guess I should ask you out on that date after all. I am nothing if not a great example of 'the wrong crowd.' Trust me."

"Oh, I know," she said with a chuckle. She looked over the balcony and her face turned serious. "But when I say 'wrong crowd,' I really mean one person in particular. And believe me when I say you've got nothing on him. But enough about that. My past is just that—mine. Nothing I want to go back to." The tone in her voice told me she had gently but firmly closed that avenue of inquiry.

"You sound like me talking about whenever somebody brings up my days on the *Braxton*."

Her eyebrows went up. "The *Braxton*? Like, the prison ship?"

"Technically," I said, repeating something the crew aboard had told us a thousand times, "the *Braxton* isn't prison. You just wish it was. How do you know the name?"

"My dad spent some time aboard when I was little. At least that's where my mom claimed he went."

"If he was a long-timer, I may have known him," I said, surprised to find myself discussing the part of my life I'd spent most of my time trying to forget.

"Nah," she said. "He only did three years or so. Once he got out, he came back home for a bit, took a job on a mining rig in the Thiessen Belt, and bit the big one in an accident about six months later."

"Shit."

She shrugged. "It happens."

Neither of us said anything for several minutes as we stared out at the city lights.

There was a slight *beep* and Carla frowned. She tapped the top of the ring she wore on her right hand and a holo message popped up, presumably from Jade. I read it over Carla's shoulder and smiled.

Your date left.

"Shit," Carla said. "What time is it?"

The holo display changed to a clock: *2138*.

She frowned at the display and tapped the top of the ring again to kill it.

"Problem?" I asked, pretending I'd been staring off the balcony the whole time instead of reading the message.

"Ah, kind of. My date left, it seems."

I snapped my fingers. "Damn. Sorry to hear that. His loss."

She shrugged. "I never liked him much anyway. He was too much of a show pony."

"What's that mean?"

"Good-looking, but not too smart, and not much fun to ride."

I laughed. "Well, I can promise you I am definitely *not* a show pony, because—"

"Are you about to tell me you're good-looking, smart, *and* fun to ride? Because I've got demonstrable proof at least two of those things aren't true."

"Well, that may be," I said with a nonchalant shrug and a sly smile. "But you'll never know about the third one unless you try, will you?"

She laughed.

"Besides, don't get too ahead of yourself there, Carla. I've got *some* sense. I'm the one who told my boss not to take your mission, remember? Your feminine wiles have no effect on me."

She laughed. "I said you were full of bullshit before, but I now proclaim you the King of Bullshit Mountain. I see the way you look at me."

"I'm an artist, Carla. I admire the feminine form," I said as seriously as I could.

"Sure thing, Snake. Whatever." She looked at the time again. "Here's the thing. I've got reservations at Chateau de Feuilles. I've never been but it's supposed to be the best food on all of Greenly. And reservations are hard as hell to get, so I don't want to waste 'em. Jade has a date tonight too, or else I'd make it a girls' night. Which leaves you, unfortunately." She smirked at me. "Unless you're too busy."

"Nope," I said, doing my best to suppress a triumphant smile. "Since you took us on the mission from hell and got the ship all shot to shit, my calendar's pretty clear. More than happy to be tonight's 'wrong crowd' you fell in with."

"Glad to hear it," she said, and led me to the elevator.

CHAPTER ELEVEN

———————————————————

Later that night, both of us tipsy from the booze and—at least in my case—the company, we shared a cab ride back to Carla's apartment building.

"So," she asked with an impish grin as she leaned against me in the back seat, "do you always make the girls pay for your food too? Is that some sort of tribal tradition in whatever backwater bumfuck place you grew up in?"

I felt my face go red. My three-hundred credits hadn't even lasted us through cocktails.

"Let me tell you a story," I said. "There's this guy—and he's already not a rich guy, okay?—but anyway, his friend meets this girl and she has this thing she wants him to do and the guy says 'no don't do it 'cause our shit's gonna get fucked up' but the guy's friend says they'll do it anyway. Then they do it and all their shit gets fucked up just like the guy said it would and so they spend like all their money trying to fix their shit but they can't 'cause their shit is too broken and the girl who asked them to do the thing only paid them a little teeny tiny bit and kept all the rest of it for herself so she could sleep on stacks of cash or whatever the fuck she does with it, while the guy and his friend drink themselves to death out of sadness 'cause their shit is fucked up. And then the girl comes along and makes fun of the guy for not having any money. The end. Sound familiar?"

Carla laughed and leaned against me. "I've heard that story, yeah. But I heard a slightly different version."

"Oh? Do tell."

"Yeah, this story is called 'The Luckiest Motherfucker in the Galaxy.' Ready?"

"Go ahead," I said.

"So, there's this lucky motherfucker who thinks he's a hell of a lot more clever than he is and he has a dumbass for a friend who agrees to do something for a smokin' hot badass who is *waaay* out of their league because the lucky motherfucker's friend wants to bone the smokin' hot badass, even though she'd rather fly her ship into an asteroid. But anyway, they somehow survive almost getting killed because they're in way over their heads and then track down the smokin' hot badass, only for the luckiest motherfucker in the galaxy to get stabbed and pass out right after the smokin' hot badass tells him how tough he is, which makes her laugh every time she thinks—"

"Hey, I'd like to see *you* try the knife to the leg thing and see how you like it," I interrupted.

"Shut up, I'm telling this story, Snake. Anyway, then the lucky motherfucker and his dumbass friend go back to their broken toys, which they blame on the smokin' hot badass even though she's the only reason they're still around. Then, for some reason the luckiest motherfucker shows up on the smokin' hot badass' doorstep and she must have not been feeling all right in the head, because she invites the luckiest motherfucker to a dinner that probably costs more than his ship, and to top it all off, actually has a really good time."

"That was a long story," I said as I gently rubbed her arm. "Does leave me with a big question, though."

She looked up at me, her smile visible in the light of passing streetlights.

"So, as the luckiest motherfucker in the galaxy, do I get lucky?"

I kissed her.

When I pulled away, she shook her head.

"He shouldn't, but he is the luckiest motherfucker in the galaxy, so probably, yeah."

Our shirts were off before we hit the next stoplight and we were sprawled out naked in the backseat of the cab the stoplight after that.

Thank God for automated cab drivers.

We managed to throw on our clothes again just in time for the cab to pull up to Carla's apartment where we ran to the elevator and proceeded to start undressing again. We ignored the elevator buzzer and gave quite a few people a shock on a floor or two, but everybody decided they could wait for the next lift. We did make it down the hall without causing too much of a scene—before we crashed into Jade's apartment, where we knocked a painting off the wall on our way over to clear whatever decorations had been on the dining room table before we made our way to the couch, then to the floor, and finally to Carla's bedroom.

———————————————-

I woke late the next morning, naked and lying next to Carla who had managed to steal the entire top sheet and blanket for herself. I had a slight hangover, but considering how good the rest of me felt, I saw no cause to complain about anything. The clock on the bedside table read *10:28.*

I stretched and yawned. The movement woke Carla, who rolled over and looked up at me.

"Aren't you cold, sleeping like that?" she asked. I looked down at my naked body. It was cold, but the shrinkage wasn't too bad.

I shrugged. "Yeah, but snakes are warm blooded, see, so they make their own heat."

Carla gave me a strange look.

"What?" I asked.

"My God, you're serious, aren't you? Snakes are *cold* blooded, dumbass, and I thought everybody knew that. I can't believe you didn't."

"Biology wasn't my strong suit in school."

"What was?"

"I didn't stick around long enough to find out."

"Now *that* I believe."

The apartment door slammed. Carla winced.

"Might want to cover up. Jade's coming, and she's gonna be on the warpath."

She tossed the blanket over me just in time for Jade to burst in the door.

"What the fuck, Carla? Last night your date shows up and he's all pissed off and makes a scene and when *my* date shows up, he thinks *your* date is upset with me and my date gets pissed off and leaves too. Then you ignore my texts all night about wanting to meet up somewhere, so I go off alone and drink myself damn near to death and wind up over at Sam's, and you *know* how that goes, so we fight again and I wind up crashing on her couch."

"Jade—"

"I'm not done yet, Carla. Then when I get in here this morning the whole place is a wreck and smells like booze and sex because you two fucked in every room in the whole goddamn place."

"We stayed out of your room, and I don't think we made it to the bathroom yet," I offered.

Jade looked at me like she wanted to claw my eyes out. "And then I come in here and find you in bed with *him*—after I told you to not bring anybody from work to the apartment. You said he was a 'business associate,' Carla. Jesus, what kind of business are you in?" Jade muttered.

"Well, I'd say this is hardly a work-related event at this point," Carla said dryly. "Call him a boyfriend if that makes you feel better."

"Makes *me* feel better," I said.

"Shut up. Nobody asked you," Jade snapped as she left the room and slammed the door behind her.

"She always like that?" I asked.

"Not always. It's a long story," Carla said. Something about her tone made me rethink a few things.

I brushed Carla's hair out of her face and kissed her again.

"Is she still upset you two broke up?"

Carla hit me with a pillow. "I told you, my past is *my* past."

———————————————

I took a long shower, made longer by the fact that Carla joined me halfway through.

We had finished brunch and Carla and I were talking about various dangerous runs we'd done before I remembered I was supposed to bring the boss back chicken wings some twenty hours ago.

"Shit," I said.

"What?"

"My boss. See, I kind of told him I was going out to pick up some wings for an early supper for us last night and it's now, uh—"

Carla checked her ring. "It's 1315."

"Okay, so I'm a *little* late."

"You said you were going out to pick up *chicken wings* and then never told him any different? How the hell did you wind up over here?"

"My brain works in very complex patterns," I said.

"When it works at all. Has he been up all night waiting for you? Worried about you?"

"My boss is not Jade. I *guarantee* you he has not been waiting up or worried. He is gonna be pissed about the wings though." A little voice in my head reminded me the wings might not be all he would be pissed about, but I ignored it.

"I'll say," Carla told me. "You're gonna earn the 'least reliable crewmember of the month' award— no doubt for the sixtieth month in a row. You'll be lucky he doesn't kick you off the crew."

"C'mon. And replace me with who, exactly? It isn't like it's the end of the world if I don't come back for a bit. Hell, this week *he* stormed off and didn't come back until four days later, hungover as shit. Besides, you're one to talk—you stood up a date last night for a guy you didn't even expect and apparently broke all your roommate's rules. And her heart. Again."

"Jade's a big girl. She can take it."

"Well, the boss is a big boy, and he can take it."

"Maybe we should get those two together," Carla said, and we both burst out laughing.

"Not a chance," I said.

"Why?" she asked. "You like him too much to subject him to Jade?"

"Nah. Other way around."

"You know," Carla observed, "he'd smack the shit out of you if he heard you say that."

"No doubt he'd try."

"But seriously, you probably ought to get back so he doesn't get too pissed," she said. "And you definitely owe him some wings."

"Yeah, yeah, I know, which is why I probably ought to get back." I stood to go.

"You two planning on heading out soon, huh?" she said with a smirk.

"Ha. You've seen the ship. What do *you* think?"

I walked to the door and was a second from stepping through it when I remembered a small but important detail. I turned back to Carla, sheepish look on my face.

"Uh, Carla, I got a little bit of a problem."

"Which is?"

"Remember the deal about me not having any money last night? 'Cause I still don't have any money. Like, none."

She gave me an incredulous look and pulled a small wad of bills from her pocket. "You are a real piece of work, asshole, you know that? I swear to God, if somebody'd told me yesterday morning I'd take *you* on a date, buy *your* food, sleep with you, and then give you *more* money for a train ride and food, I think I'd have had them committed." She slapped the money into my palm with feigned exasperation. "Don't spend it all in one place."

"Thanks," I said. "I won't."

"I wasn't kidding last night—you really are the luckiest motherfucker in the whole world right now, and you had better not forget it," she said from the table as the apartment door closed behind me.

"Yeah, I know," I whispered to myself as I strode down the hallway, a spring in my step.

CHAPTER TWELVE

———————————————————————————————————— ►

I walked up the open cargo bay ramp and into the Black Sun 490, plastic bag with a box of wings and a pair of cold beers in my left hand. My boss looked up from where he sat next to a wiring diagram and a mess of circuit boards. He seemed surprised to see me, and I think his first reaction was relief, but it transitioned to anger in an eyeblink.

"What the fuck?"

"A funny thing happened on the way to the wing place," I said as I sat the box of wings and beers down. "It took me a little longer than expected."

"You don't say." He gave me an icy glare. "Here I was figuring you'd gone and got yourself hired on somewhere else and then you show back up with chicken wings fifteen hours later or whatever, looking like the happiest motherfucker alive? Where the hell have you been?"

I sat down on the couch and stretched my feet out. "It's a long story, really."

He gestured to the battered ship. "I got nothing but time, Snake. Nothing but time. So, start talking." He opened the box of wings and a beer and leaned against the computer cabinet.

Even though I'd been thinking about it the entire time on the train, I still hadn't figured out how to tell him anything without this seeming like a repeat of the Nasra incident, only a million times worse.

"So, on the way to the wing place, I stopped to light a cigarette over near one of the apartment complexes because the wind was blowing and—"

"*Snake*," the boss said.

"Fine. I noticed one of the apartment numbers on a sign. It was seven digits, like the number Carla left us, which got me thinking maybe it was an apartment number."

"What does that have to do with anything?"

"A *loan*, Boss. Remember? She told us at Joey Machete's that if we needed a loan, she could talk terms."

"She wasn't being serious, dumbass. She was making fun of us."

"I know, I know, and that's what I thought too, but I figured what the hell I might as well try. It's got to be better than borrowing money from the Sevens or flying without radiation shields or whatever, right? So, I took the train to the apartment, which turned out to be her roommate's. But anyway, Carla was there so I went to ask her for the loan, but it didn't quite go like I planned and we got to talking."

"About the loan?"

"About a bunch of stuff, really. Anyway, so—"

"Okay," my boss cut me off. "So enough about Carla's. Then what?"

"What do you mean 'then what?'" I asked.

"I mean *what happened after you left Carla's*? What the fuck do you think I mean?"

"Well, that question is more complicated than you probably think, because—"

"Jesus, Snake, just get to the point and tell me what the fuck is going on."

Fine. He asked for it, didn't he?

"Okay, look, here's the deal. After Carla and I got to talking we wound up going out to someplace she had reservations to—fancy place, Chapeau de something or other. Anyway, after that…" I trailed off.

He very deliberately sat his beer bottle down and calmly folded his arms across his chest, a mixture of complete disbelief and burning rage on his face. His lower jaw worked, and I could almost hear his teeth grinding.

"And then?"

"Look, man," I said. "What do you want? Do you want me to tell you we fucked in the cab, and then in the elevator and then on the wall and the table and the couch and the floor and the bed? And then woke up this morning and did it again in the shower, and it was for sure the best, most absolutely mind-blowing sex I've ever had? Because that's pretty much the 'and then' portion of the story. Is that what you wanted to hear?"

"No, Snake. That is actually the *very last* thing I wanted to hear this morning. Very last. Like, I almost would have rather read my own obituary."

"Well, you asked," I said. "And now you know."

"Did you get it?" he asked in a quiet voice.

"Get what?"

"The loan, you dumb motherfucker. The *loan*—the whole reason you went over there, remember?"

His question hit me like a punch in the face.

Shit.

"Actually, it never came up."

He didn't say anything. Instead, he folded the box of wings closed and set it back in the plastic bag. He sat the bag just inside the computer cabinet and looked up at me from the floor, his face completely without emotion.

"Snake, my hands are greasy. Which is why I am going to stand up and wash my hands and dry them *real* good, because I don't want to lose my grip. Then, I'm going to grab that big, heavy, adjustable crescent wrench we have and break every motherfucking bone in your whole goddamn body. After that, I will fly your lifeless corpse out to one of those cannibal death cults in the Akula Nebula, where I will let them eat you. Then, I'll make sure that when they shit you out, they put your remains in little plastic baggies I can personally take with me as I travel the galaxy and leave on distant planets, so that the entire fucking universe can understand, ultimately, that you are a giant piece of shit."

"Hey, man, I got you the wings, didn't I?"

———————————

I worked outside on the hull the rest of the afternoon, preparing engine one for removal. There were a couple reasons why I felt this was the best use of my time, the main one being that I figured the harder I was to reach, the less likely the boss would be to snap and choke the ever-living shit out of me. The second reason was that to unbolt engine one from its mount, I had to use the big adjustable crescent wrench, which seemed best for me to keep out of his hands—just in case.

"*Stupid. Goddamn. Motherfucking. Bastard. Bitch,*" I grunted as I struggled with the number five bolt on the starboard side, pulling as hard as I could on the wrench handle, but the bolt refused to loosen. I wiped the sweat off my forehead and checked the bolt head again, as if looking at it would somehow make it do something that putting a wrench to it and swearing wouldn't.

"This thing is stuck, Boss," I called down from atop the ship. "It won't budge."

He stepped out from the hold and gave me the evil eye from the cargo ramp.

I rolled my eyes. "C'mon, man," I said. "Let all that stuff from this morning go. I'm trying to actually get some shit done here, how about a little help?"

"Fine."

He disappeared inside and came back a moment later, holding the meter-long heavy steel pipe we used to slide over the wrench handle for more leverage. "You're probably gonna need the breaker bar," he said with a wicked grin. "Come on down here and get it." He slapped it into the palm of his left hand.

"You know what?" I asked. "I think I can get it with the wrench after all. Thanks for the help."

"No, no," he said with mock politeness. "Anything I can do to make your life easier. Helping you work on things, buying all the food, being your divining rod for women, whatever you need."

"A divining rod?"

"Old tool for finding where to drill for water. In our case, it means *I* find the girls, and apparently *you* do the drilling."

"Look, man, you gotta learn to let things go."

"Oh, there's all kinds of things I'm thinking about letting go," he answered, staring daggers at me.

A silver, late-model SUV rolled across the taxiway and pulled up next to our pad. The windows were tinted too dark for me to tell who our visitor was, but in my experience, this sort of entrance did not bode well.

Atop the ship, I looked over the edge and tensed, wondering if I could jump from the roof to the concrete pad without breaking my legs in the event of gunfire. My boss didn't drop the breaker bar completely, but he did shift it to his left hand to free up his gun hand, which he rested on the butt of his revolver.

The engine cut off and the two front doors opened. Jade stepped out of the driver's seat, closed her door, and leaned against it, arms crossed and a look on her face that told me Carla was pushing the limits of her patience. Carla hopped out of the passenger seat, back in her familiar flight suit. When she noticed me atop the ship and the boss on the ground with the breaker bar, her face broke out in a wide grin.

"So, I see things are going well," she said.

"*Carla*," my boss said in a voice usually reserved for discussion of communicable diseases.

"What are you doing up there?" she called to me in a mocking tone. "I didn't know snakes could climb ladders."

"If properly motivated, snakes can do all kinds of things," I answered.

"Cut the bullshit, Carla, what do you want? Aside from Snake, for some reason?" the boss said.

"Well, I figured you two would still be here—heh heh—but I wanted to chat with Snake a bit before I flew out. I got a surprise hot job from Mr. Tanaka."

I frowned. It wasn't entirely unexpected, but I had been looking forward to a few more days.

"Well, there he is," the boss said, pointing at me with the breaker bar. "Bye."

"Man, you are pretty damn bitter, aren't you?" she asked him.

"Look, if all you came by for was to rub my face in the shit you got us into, get lost, okay Carla? I don't care if you and Snake are whatever it is you two are, but I don't have to put up with shit from you."

Carla gave a nonchalant shrug.

"Fortunately for you, ace, I've taken a liking to your gunner, which is why I was thinking about something he'd said last night."

"And what was that?"

She ignored him and looked up at me instead. "You never actually told me why you came by, Snake. I asked but we got sidetracked talking about other things and then, by… *doing* other things—"

Jade interrupted with a loud, contemptuous snort.

"Anyway," Carla continued, "I got to thinking about it and I realized what you actually came for. You came for a loan."

I nodded. "Yep. I remembered you made a comment about loan terms in Joey Machete's. I didn't figure it would work, but what the hell, right?"

"And I take it you still need it, right? And that—" Carla asked.

"You are about the absolute last person I'd want to borrow money from," my boss said through clenched teeth.

"Well, don't worry about it, then, 'cause I wasn't going to offer *you* anything. I came to talk to Snake, remember?" She looked up at me.

"So, do you need it or not?" she asked me.

I felt the boss's eyes boring into the side of my head, but I didn't meet them. Instead, I looked down at our scarred, scuffed, shot-up Black Sun 490.

"Yeah, we still need it."

"How much?"

I looked down at the boss, whose body language told me he'd finally accepted the inevitable. "We need forty grand," he said with a sigh.

"Forty grand it is then, Carla," I said.

She gave a low whistle. "That's a lot of fuckin' money. What's this bucket of bolts worth, anyway? One hundred? One-fifteen, tops? Anyway, I can't loan you forty. But I can do thirty-five."

I looked to the boss, who nodded. "Okay, we'll take it."

"There is no *we* here, Snake. This is a loan to *you*," she said with a quick wink in my direction when my companion wasn't looking. "And that's the thing. You have zero collateral."

Her wink told me she was up to something, but I had no idea what. Whatever it was, the boss was way ahead of me. His brow furrowed and he appeared to be working something out in his head.

"Sixty-forty," he told Carla.

She laughed. "His way, maybe."

"How? You just said it's worth one-fifteen," he protested.

"I don't see a whole long line of people out here ready to buy you out, do you?"

"Fine, then, an even fifty-fifty," he muttered. "But the liability is *his*, got it? So, if you decide to take it out in blood, it's on him, okay?"

"What good does that do me?" Carla asked. "If I come for something, I'll come for the collateral, which would mean half. Take it or leave it," she said with an infuriating smile.

"I hate the both of you so much," he groused. "I see why you two hit it off. You're perfect for each other."

"Can somebody explain what's going on?" I called from atop the ship.

"Carla just twisted your poor boss's arm to make you half owner of the ship to secure the loan," Jade said from her position leaning against the SUV. "Jesus, you *are* dumb, aren't you?"

My boss pointed at her. "You know what? I don't know you, but you—*you*—are a voice of reason. I like you."

"Thanks," Jade said with a nod in his direction.

Carla and I shared a knowing look.

Not fucking likely, admittedly. But maybe. For a little while.

"So, wait. Now I'm half owner of the ship?" I asked, amazed. I'd never owned anything that wouldn't fit in a duffle bag.

"Technically, I am, until you pay me back," Carla corrected me.

"Speaking of which, what exactly are the repayment terms?" I asked.

She shrugged. "Get it back to me when you can. And check in every once in a while."

"As co-owner of the ship, I'm sure I can make that happen," I said, with a taunting look at the boss.

"I swear on the cosmos, I will drop your ass off in the middle of the desert on Ranier if you keep on like that," he threatened.

"Please do," Jade said, earning her a dirty look from Carla.

"But let's see it on paper before I hand over a cashcard," Carla told my boss. "Fetch the title."

Grumbling, he disappeared into the ship while I climbed down to the ground.

"You really are the luckiest motherfucker in the world. Do you realize we spent the whole night together and you never mentioned the loan? Not even once?" Carla asked.

"I had other things on my mind."

"I bet you did." She gave me a playful shove.

The boss reappeared, ship's title in its plastic book. I realized I had never seen it before and didn't recognize any of the names of previous owners on the document besides my boss's. I signed next to his above the spot marked *Co-owner* ___ *Percent*, and he wrote *50* in the blank, initialing underneath it.

Carla tugged on her flight suit zipper and withdrew a cashcard. She used her ring to transfer thirty-five thousand credits to it and handed it to me.

I took it and turned to my boss—*partner*. "Boss," I said. "We're back in business." I thought for a second. "Do I still have to call you 'Boss' even though I—"

"Yes," he interrupted. "Yes, you do. You may be part owner of the ship on paper, but I'm still the captain."

Carla shrugged. "That's fair, honestly."

"Thanks for the support," he muttered.

I chuckled and clapped him on the back. "Don't sweat it, Boss. I've been saying it so long anyway, I wouldn't know what else to call you."

Carla's ring beeped and she checked the time.

"Shit. I gotta go, but before I do, I got a tip for you—actually two," she said to my partner. "And I'm going give them to you, even though you're an ungrateful bastard."

"Oh, boy," he said sarcastically. "I can't *wait* to hear what you've got for me."

"Good, so listen up. Tip one: Mr. Tanaka has special runs he needs done occasionally. These are not Tanaka Corporation runs. These are more… personal sorts of things, and they pay well. Anyway, he never reuses a shipper to haul his personal cargo so nobody can get a full picture of what's going on. He'll be looking for another crew in two weeks and I put in a good word to him about you guys. Go to Joey's and ask for Lei Ming and tell her Carla sent you. She'll hook you up."

His mouth dropped open. I could tell he'd expected her to give him some more smartass "life advice." To be honest, so did I.

"Uh, well, thanks, I guess—really," he said. "What's the second tip?"

"Never trust a pretty face."

That's what I was expecting.

"Yeah. Thanks for that too, Carla. Don't you have somewhere to be?"

Carla laughed. "Yeah, I do. Anyway, take care of Snake for me, would ya?"

"Somebody has to," he muttered.

"And, Snake," she said to me, her green eyes dazzling in the first sunset, "see you around. Soon."

I nodded. "Yeah."

CHAPTER THIRTEEN

Two weeks later, we sat on the taxiway, exhausted from long hours and backbreaking work, but at least it was done.

"Black Sun 490. Greenly Space Control clears you off LZ 5 for flight corridor bravo. You are go for takeoff," the controller's voice said over the comms.

In my turret, I couldn't help but smile.

"Roger, Greenly Control," the boss said.

He engaged the retro-rockets and we leapt off the pad, punching through the low cloud cover and into the brightness of Greenly's twin suns above. He banked the ship left and right to make sure it maneuvered as expected.

"Everything looking good up there, Boss?" I called up to the cockpit as we ascended, the bright sky giving way to deeper blues and blacks of the high atmosphere. "I'm showing all normal readings down here, but I got a little static on the targeting display."

"It's used. What do you expect?"

"Fair enough."

"Switching to primary engines," he called. Our Black Sun 490 shuddered as the engines roared and we punched out of the atmosphere into space.

"Well, I guess our test procedures were good and we did the work generally right," I said as he steered us toward the nav lane.

"Well, we're alive now, but let's wait and see if the heat shields hold up during reentry before we start celebrating," he cracked. "Now *that* would be an unpleasant—"

Thunk.

A square piece of metal from somewhere well forward of the turret tumbled past my station and streaked bright as it burned up in the Greenly atmosphere.

"Yo, man, did you tighten down the P1 access panel?" I asked.

"No. You said you were gonna do it, remember?"

I sighed, because as soon as he brought it up, I did remember.

"Shit."

DAVID DIXON

Snake and the Boss
will return in...

SIX-GUN SHUFFLE

Snake and the boss have made a lot of enemies, but up until their trip to Yaeger, they've never had any beef with Michael Ver, the galaxy's most bankable popstar—mainly because they haven't met him yet. After Ver's security steals the boss's coat during a video shoot, he drags Snake into Ver's inner circle to get it back. The boss teaches Ver a lesson about the difference between looking tough and being tough, and when video of the incident leaks, he finds himself a minor viral video star. His fame wins him a lot of free drinks, and even better, catches the eye of a gorgeous redhead named Kell. Things are looking up.

Looking up, that is, until Kell goes missing and the boss goes after her. After a shootout with Ver's crew, things go from bad to worse—nobody can find Ver, and Snake and the boss are the prime suspects in his disappearance. They decide to get off Yaeger while they can, but when they catch Ver's head of security trying to steal their ship after he's loaded his own cargo in the hold, they realize they've stumbled into the sort of scheme that's impossible to run from.

The next thing they know they've got a bounty on their heads and hardly a friend in sight. Carla and Kell are the only people they can count on, but Snake is starting to think that Kell knows more than she's letting on. They can only play with the hand they're dealt, but has Kell been playing a different game all along? It's a mixed-up tale of bounty hunters, crooked cops, popstars and... insurance agents?... in *Six-Gun Shuffle*.

SIX-GUN SHUFFLE
TEASER

You ever noticed how something can seem small and insignificant when it starts and then— *boom*—the next thing you know that little speck of light behind you is a missile screaming right for your ass? Life is like that a lot for the boss and me, it seems. One minute something is a minor inconvenience and the next minute it's a matter of life and death.

We were at Holloway Spaceport on Yaeger VII, having just completed a run from Piker's Distillery on Talos. We'd gotten confirmation that our payment had come through, so we trudged across the icy, windblown spaceport toward our beat-up Black Sun 490.

I took a worried glance at the sky. Overhead, massive black clouds churned like my stomach after too many White Russians. The locals had warned us that the coming storm would snow the whole city in for two or three days, if not more. While ordinarily I wouldn't have minded a break from the confines of the ship for a bit, Yaeger VII was hardly the place to do it. The only thing Yaeger VII was known for was a few second-rate casinos, shitty weather, bad beer, and obnoxious locals. Kinda reminded me of New New England. I scowled and fished a cigarette out of my shirt pocket.

The boss watched me light it and gave me that grin he has when he thinks he's about to be clever. "Man, Snake, you sure are smoking a lot these days."

I snorted. "I've always smoked."

"Yeah, but it seems like it's more here of late. When we left Greenly, you smoked like a chimney until we ran into Carla on Tayir. And you practically quit while we were on Rucker Watson's with her, and as soon as we left you started back up again. I think they're like your replacement for Carla."

I took a drag before I answered. "At least I've got someone to replace."

His grin disappeared.

I clapped him on the back. "Better luck next time, champ."

"Have I ever mentioned how much I hate you?" the boss replied.

I shrugged. "Maybe, but I probably wasn't listening."

"Hey, Snake, there's a pair of guys hanging out beside the ship," the boss said, suddenly serious. He nodded to the starboard side of the ship a hundred meters away, where a pair of men stood in the shadow of our Black Sun 490 looking up at the sky. My gut tightened. They were probably just using it as shelter against the wind, but in our line of work, you could never be too careful.

As we drew closer, the boss tucked his hands under his arms, which to someone else might make it seem like he was just keeping them warm, but I knew he had his right hand on the grip of the .45 revolver tucked in his shoulder holster.

A roar passing overhead made me flinch, and I looked up to see a large ducted hovercraft coming in low. The pilot flared the engines, which sent icy wind and stinging pellets of ice flying. He landed too close to our ship, and as the boss and I stared in outrage, the side door dropped open and half a dozen more men stepped out, sauntering onto the spaceport tarmac like they owned the place. One of them actually *leaned* up against our Black Sun 490, a move that in the spacer world is the sort of etiquette violation that would normally earn you anywhere from a broken nose to a bullet in the brainpan, depending on how far out in the Fringe you were.

The boss and I stomped toward the ship. My blood was boiling. What kind of asshole thought he had the right to just walk up to our shit and lean on it like he was the goddamned UNF General Secretary or something? Did these clowns have a death wish?

"Yo, dipshit," the boss shouted across the frozen spaceport. "Touch my ship again and see what happens."

The man who'd leaned against it leapt away like he'd been shocked. By now we were close enough to see that they were dressed in the sort of expensive cold weather gear meant to go ice climbing on Titan or something but usually used to keep super rich pricks from suffering even the smallest amount of dick shrinkage.

"*Excuse* me?" one of the men snapped. "Are you talking to *us*? Who the fuck do you think you are? Who gave you permission to be here?"

"'Who gave *you* permission?' is the question, because last time I checked, I didn't give you permission to touch shit," the boss growled as we drew closer.

"We're here for the video shoot, and we rented the whole spaceport," the man huffed. "Everything here is supposed to be available for use."

"Well, you've been misinformed," I answered. "This is our ship, and it's not available for whatever the fuck you think it is. So, you got like, *maybe* five seconds to clear out before things get ugly."

"I think there's been some sort of misunderstanding," he replied.

"Five," I said as I took another menacing step closer to the ship. I'd been in the game long enough to know that these were the type who'd never even match the ante, much less stick around for the call.

"But I—"

"Four," the boss said, slapping his fist into his palm.

"Can't we just—"

"Three," I said, sighing as I flicked my cigarette away.

The men scampered toward the hovercraft. The boss and I dropped the cargo ramp and strolled inside, chuckling.

Fucking earthworms—the same on every planet.

We got to work doing maintenance, as always. I worked inside, topping off fluid levels, replacing scrubber filters in the life support system, and recalibrating my turret servos. The boss worked outside, running down an intermittent fault in the J7 junction box that kept shorting out our gravimetric sensor every time the shield generator cycled.

He walked back up the cargo ramp ten minutes later, soaked in sweat and without his coat, muttering curses under his breath. I looked up from the left side scrubber bank. "What's up?" I asked.

"Fucking J7 cover is stuck."

"Yeah. It was that same way the last time I worked on it. I think the locking ring is busted.

You're probably going to have to pry it off, and that'll mean we—"

One of the men from earlier appeared at the base of the ramp, careful not to actually set foot on the cargo ramp itself. He cleared his throat.

The boss turned to face him, but before either one of us could tell the guy to get lost, another man joined him. This second guy was no rich asshole—redundant, I know—in five thousand credits worth of winter gear. He was a hulking bruiser in black boots, jeans, and only a long-sleeved T-shirt despite the fact that the first few snowflakes had already begun to fall. This was the type of guy who wouldn't just see the ante, but might even raise it.

"See, Liz," the man from earlier said to his new friend, "these are the two I was talking about."

Liz looked up the ramp at us, and I got the feeling he was sizing us up. I took a drag from my cigarette and tried to be nonchalant. In this business, sometimes it's best just to let folks sort out for themselves who they're dealing with.

"You giving my man a hard time?" Liz finally said.

The boss shrugged. "Not really. But if your man comes over here touching our shit again, he might get one."

Liz nodded. "I get you, but here's the thing: you're not supposed to be here."

My expression didn't change, but something about the way Liz spoke set little warning alarms chiming in my head. He had the sort of quiet, steely confidence that only came from having been here before—and coming out on top.

"I got a paid invoice for three hundred credits for the use of this pad and utilities that says otherwise," the boss said.

Liz shook his head. "I don't care if you got a paid invoice for fucking Mars. We paid for the whole spaceport. For a video shoot."

Liz casually slid up his left sleeve to reveal a brilliant red lizard tattoo, and suddenly the reason for the "Liz" nickname clicked into place—*Liz* for "lizard." A half a second later, something else clicked into place for me. That tattoo, like the snake coiled around my left arm, wasn't just there for decoration. It was a gang sign, which in this case meant he either had been or still was a member of the Iguanas, a sector gang that ran Z on the regular and occasionally pulled side gigs as "personal protection."

Fuck.

Beside me, the boss flared his nostrils. "But like I said, we already paid for the pad, and I'm not paying for another. We got maintenance to do. But you let us finish up our shit here, and we'll be glad to get gone. We weren't planning on sticking around anyway."

Liz flicked his eyes to the man who'd told us to move the first time. With Liz by his side, he'd regained some of his earlier rich asshole confidence. He shook his head. "No way, Liz. We're behind a day already, and camera and crew time is running the company four grand a minute. Michael is already unhappy with how things are going, and I need him in a good mood for the video. I want them gone."

Liz looked back at us. "You heard him."

"We already paid for the pad," the boss protested. "Call station control. They can't just—"

Liz chuckled wickedly. "Go ahead. Call 'em."

Holloway Center Control, of course, sided with Liz, giving us some story about how buried deep in the standard twenty-page rental contract was some bullshit clause about "terms and conditions subject to change without notice."

"So, there you go," Liz said after our ten-minute argument with Holloway Center Control. "Get lost."

"And if I say no?" the boss asked, his hand resting on his pistol.

"I'll call station security out here and they can move you, if you want to go the hard way," Liz said with a shrug. "They're good friends of mine, but they're not very careful people. Something would probably get broken, and I don't think you want that."

The boss and I exchanged a glance, and I hoped he could read in my look that this was a fight we probably wouldn't win. I don't mind dragging things out as a matter of principle, but I also don't like doing any more maintenance than I have to—on the ship or my face.

"You know what? Fuck this," the man with Liz said. "We're wasting time, and if the weather gets too bad, I'm going to have to delay the shoot *again*. Let them stay, for all I care. I'll edit their piece-of-shit rust bucket out in post." He looked at us and narrowed his eyes. "Just close the cargo bay, and you can have your precious pad back when we finish. But you have *got* to stay inside. If one of you comes out and fucks up my shot, I'm going to have station security move your ship *and* I'll sue you for every fucking credit you've got, you hear me?"

The boss's jaw worked, but he nodded. "We'll stay inside, but don't touch anything out there, you got it? This ship may be a 'piece-of-shit rust bucket,' but it's *my* piece-of-shit rust bucket."

I decided now was not the time to point out that *technically*, the ship was half mine, too.

"Sure, whatever," the man said with a dismissive wave, and he and Liz disappeared back out onto the tarmac.

——————————————-

Five hours later, it was almost dark and we were almost crazy. It turns out the video shoot was for a music holo, and whatever song they were shooting for either only had four words—*baby, baby, baby, baby*—repeated over and over again, or they shot the same goddamn scene a hundred times. Either way, by the time they were done, if I heard one more *baby* I was going to put a pistol in my mouth.

As soon as their hovercraft took off, passing overhead and shaking the ship, the boss and I went outside to stretch our legs. The air was cold like a knife between the ribs, and it was all I could do to smoke without feeling like my fingers were going to freeze off.

The boss clapped his bare arms around himself for warmth and disappeared around the front of the ship, only to return a moment later, glancing across the empty docking pads.

"Where's my coat?" he asked.

"The black one? How the fuck should I know? I'm not your mom, man."

"I left it out front, on top of the toolbox next to the J7 box."

"Maybe it blew across the—"

"No. I looped it through the handle. Plus, it'd be blowing around out here if the wind got it."

I shivered against the cold. "I dunno, boss. If you left it there, it should still be there."

A sudden look of fury crossed his face. "I'll bet one of that piece-of-shit film crew took it! I *told* him not to touch our stuff. If I see somebody wearing it, I'm going to break their goddamn arms."

I snorted. "Dude. Why would somebody steal your nasty-ass old coat?" I asked. "But whatever, it doesn't matter. I think we got another—"

"I don't want another coat, damn it! I want mine. And I wanna know who took it."

I gave him an incredulous look. "It's just a coat, man. If you want another one, I know we're hard up for cash, but I think we can afford a *coat*. It isn't like that thing was the height of fashion anyway."

He stomped up the ramp. "That coat has sentimental value."

"Sentimental value?" I asked, following him. "You shitting me right now?"

"No, I'm serious. When I got this ship, only two things came with it." He pointed to the .45 revolver hanging in its shoulder rig by the hatch to the crew compartment. "The first was that pistol. The second was the coat. Now they're my pistol and my coat. And I want my damn coat."

"You're wrong. *Three* things came with the ship. That pistol, that coat, and a fuckton of headaches," I cracked.

"Goddamnit, Snake, I'm serious. I want my fucking coat back."

"Well, I got no idea where it went, all right? But if I see it, I'll make sure to tell it to come home and that daddy misses it very much."

I chuckled at his scowl.

"Look," the boss said. "I get that you can't get it right now, because your tiny little reptile brain is incapable of understanding how somebody else might feel, but let me put it in terms you can understand. How long have you had that ratty green duffel bag you always carry around with you?"

"I dunno, as long as I can remember. At least since I was ten or twelve, 'cause whenever me and my mom got kicked out of a place, that's what I put all my stuff in when we left."

"Okay, fine. So, say somebody stole your duffel bag, what—"

"Nobody's gonna steal my duffel bag," I objected.

"Jesus, Snake! Work with me. Say somebody did steal it, because—somehow—they were even worse off than you. If somebody sketched that bag from you, what would you do?"

I gave it a moment's thought before I answered. "I'd fuck 'em right up."

"Right. Same thing with my coat."

"Whatever, bossman. If we're out and about and you see somebody with your coat on, I guess I'll give you a hand, if it means that much to you." I shook my head and went back to working on the voltage calculations I'd abandoned earlier, figuring I'd heard the last I'd ever hear about his stupid coat.

I was wrong, of course.

About the Author

David Dixon has been writing fiction and non-fiction for over twenty years. A husband, father of two, and Army veteran whose combat days are long behind him, he lives in Northern Virginia where he writes across a variety of genres and topics. He believes that for every person and every place, there's a story, whether it's a comedy, tragedy, or something in between—and it's his hope to write them all.

More From Dark Brew Press

Urban Gothic
by Stephen Coghlan

Burned out and drugged up, Alec LeGuerrier spends his days faking it, barely ekeing out an existence while living in a haze of confusion and medicated mellowness. That is, until he stops a gang of nightmarish oddities from killing a strange young woman with indigo eyes.

Dragged into the lands of the dreaming, he must come to terms with his brutal past and his grim imagined future in a land his body knows is real, but his mind refuses to acknowledge.

The Cranes of Blackwell by J.D. Kellner

Bergden and Alyssa Crane are dutiful citizens of the Regime. Bergden, a Regime blackjack and Alyssa, a faithful wife, do what they can to provide for their son, James even when it means sacrificing their very freedom. But when Bergden is accused of treason, the Cranes must flee for their lives to escape the terrible reach of the Regime. During the escape, Bergden and Alyssa become separated.

Now, Bergden and Alyssa will do whatever they must, and against all odds, to unite their family. With the tyrannical Chancellor Kroft hunting them night and day, both must discover their inner strengths to conquer their fears and find each other's arms.

Little do they realize that a greater threat lurks in the shadows.

Printed in Great Britain
by Amazon